THOUGHTS
- and DASHES

George Manus

2. edition

Author: George Manus
Copyright: George Manus
Design and layout: Ole Praud
Vignettes: Morten Løfberg
Copyright Dashes and front page: Jan Arnt

Print: BoD - Books on Demand, Norderstedt, Germany
Editor: BoD - Books on Demand, Copenhagen, Denmark (BoD.dk)
email george.manus@maxmanus.com

Other books written by George Manus.

TANKER - og Tankestreker, Norwegian

REFLECTIONS I, English
REFLEKSJONER I, Norwegian

REFLECTIONS II, English
REFLEKSJONER II, Norwegian

REFLECTIONS III, English
REFLEKSJONER III, Norwegian

A WOMAN'S MANY MIGRATIONS, English
EN KVINNES MANGE FLYTTINGER. Norwegian

INNOVATIONS AND CREATIONS, English

70 YEARS IN COMMUNICATION- about the MAX MANUS Companies, English
70 ÅR I KOMMUNIKASJON - om MAX MANUS firmaene, Norwegian

2017

ISBN No: 9788771884081

Foreword

These "THOUGHTS", from the first 51 days of 2001, are dedicated to my daughter, Anne-Marie.

It might just as well have been only a few days and why it ended up being 51 and didn't continue, was probably because no plans were ever made for anything more than just putting a few "THOUGHTS" on paper.

I think it must have been other engagements which made them stop where they did. My writing was replaced by other activities such as putting ideas into inventions and subsequent production.

Anyway, it was not always easy to find time to write, for even though the "THOUGHTS" themselves were short and spontaneous, they were written on the actual day they happened.

The "THOUGHTS" were written in Cabrera in the South of Spain where we lived at the time, apart from the ones made when I was in Norway in connection with business.

I had, when these "THOUGHTS" were written, long since completed my "REFLECTIONS I" which had just been laid aside.

Now, some sixteen years later, the time has come to tidy up my writings with the idea in mind that perhaps some friends, acquaintances and others might like to have a look at them.

"THOUGHTS" were at the time written in English, and is now being published with the title "THOUGHTS - and Dashes", together with my other books.

I thank Anne Schild for her help with the language, Morten Løfberg for his vignettes, Jan Arnt for his Dashes and front page and my friend Ole Praud for his invaluable consultancy work.

The South of Spain,
2017
George Manus

george.manus@maxmanus.com

The Diversity of Dashes

For years – ever since I was a little boy – I have been drawing simple little dashes whenever I'm sitting about doing nothing. Early on I discovered that one's thoughts flourish when one draws dashes – and the other way around. Early on I also discovered that a line can be drawn in many different ways and that a thin little line immediately comes to life, if one ends it with a little dip or a little jump. Two jumps makes one think of hills or perhaps of a woman's breasts. One line and two dots make a face which, by the way, one can vary ad infinitum.

You yourself can try drawing a line and two dots ten times in a row, and you'll see that no two are the same and, not least, that you've had a lot of new thoughts going through your mind in the process.

A short line is the simplest form of drawing. If one adds one wavy line, however, it reminds one of water, and seven wavy lines can make one think of an entire ocean.

If one draws lines in different directions like, for example, in a spider-web, then one's mind starts thinking thoughts – or thought-spinning, as I call it.

The web is a work of art but also a predator's trap, which holds on tight to the prey, making it suffer a long slow death until the spider takes pity on it and eats it – skin and all.

If one puts pencil to paper and starts drawing in a criss-cross pattern, structures often appear. Sometimes it's just a mess, but other times one can see crooked or geometric structures and creatures: HEY, isn't that a woman, a man, a clown, an animal or something completely different.

Then one's thoughts follow the movement of the pencil or the brush and suddenly the lines turn into a VISUAL THOUGHT. Too fancy a word, which is why we in everyday speech only call it an illustration.

Sometimes we give the dash a title, which supports what the eye can see. Other times we play around with the title and give the work itself a name, so that one as viewer asks: HEY … why that title? And after some afterthought the viewer starts asking, if that's what he really means, and then often sees new things in the motif.

Most often the little dash end up in a drawer somewhere and the best ones perhaps on a wall under glass and with a pretty frame around them.

Or in a book about THOUGHTS, where they provide the opportunity for pauses and afterthoughts.

Happy viewing.

Jan Arnt Architect MAA – Denmark 2017

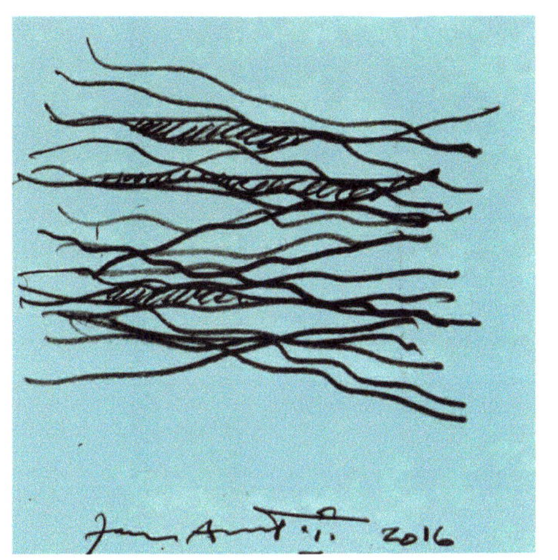

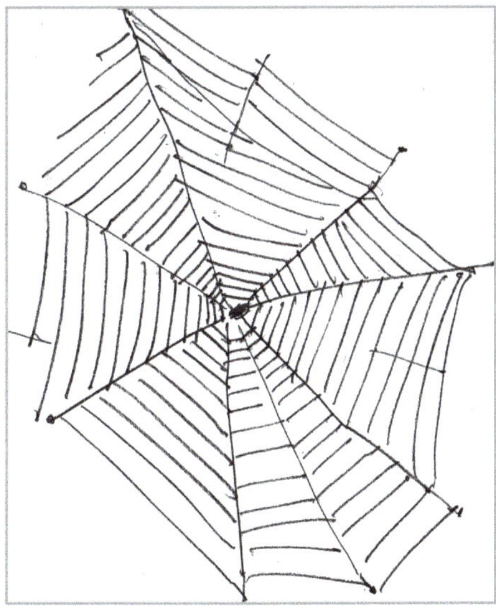

Waves
Fantasy
Weave

Jan Arnt 2017

A short a long
A triangle, and a rod,
A bell that says Ding-Dang
A clock, a wall, a man
That is angry
A man who is angry
A wall, a clock
a short a long
A triangle, and a rod
A bell that says Ding-Dang.

Tradition

The fact that it is the first of January, meaning the first day of a new year, is always a bit special, providing of course that you have a good feeling about the ending of the old year. Or is that necessarily so? For many it may also be a relief to leave the past year behind and to start a new one from scratch.

Whatever way you look at it, there is something very fascinating about a book with 365 unprinted pages. One thing is for sure, the past year is already history, and what the new one will bring, no one can foresee. A number of assumptions can be made, but with very doubtful accuracy. It is 15 degrees Celsius in the air and the sun is shining from a blue sky.

This in itself is nothing very special, as most of the days here are sunny throughout the year.

Southern Spain, of course, about half an hour's drive from the Mediterranean sea into the mountains of Cabrera.

If you want to find this place don't ask for the hot, posh places, but seek information from people who have already decided that this is the place to live.

No two houses alike, small ones or big ones, they all fit beautifully into the landscape wherever they are placed, or rather designed.

The architectural blend is a mixture of Andalucian and Moorish style, and to avoid making them "stick out", they are all painted different shades of terracotta.

When you have been away for a while, like we have for the last week which we spent in the western part of Andalucia, and you drive up the mountain side to your Shangri-La, it really gives you peace of mind to think about the fact that you have chosen the right place to live.

I am, however, very pleased that people have different tastes and desires.

Our strategy, at least as things look today, is to build between ten and twenty houses per year in the Urbanization.

These daily "thoughts" should not generally refer so much to places as events, they should be short and just concentrate on those happenings which will be worth remembering when a new day starts and the past one becomes history.

It is already a tradition that we play golf on January the first, and so also this year.

A couple of birdies, or not to mention a hole in one, would more than qualify for making the day's "up", while playing badly would not qualify for a "down" unless it was a total disaster.

The reason for not making a "down" out of my bad play is, of course, because it happens rather too often and therefore would become too much of a repetition.

Nothing in the vicinity of birdies or a hole in one happened, nor was my play disastrous, so no qualification was achieved.

Apart from that we had a wonderful day on the course.

It is always important to find an excuse for your imprecise playing, but normally it would just remain an excuse, and seldom be related to facts.

O.K., my back is hurting more than it has for a long time, and that is where the "up" comes in.

Back home, the Jacuzzi, which takes a good half an hour to fill, was prepared while the fire in the lounge was lit.

My wife prepared a couple of glasses of champagne and some crackers with foie gras, leftover from the early days of Christmas.

With only my head above the water and its circulation gently hammering my body, a wonderful peace and good feeling comes to me on this first day of the new year.

With peace in my soul, I grab my Pocket Memo, the words of which I will convert into this text, knowing that I later, when reading it, will be able to bring back the wonderful feeling of the "ups" on this, the first day of the year 2001.

CD carousel

I have always believed that when things go wrong they really do. I will not here touch on the subject of how I at times get a feeling that my own mood can influence the stability of my computer. Surely there will come a day when I will write about that. Nothing is wrong with the computer, but with a much more down-to-earth couple of machines.

I have a lovely wife who serves me a cup of tea in bed every morning.

She could today, when returning with the cups, tell me that the dishwasher had been running all night without responding to the program. It is not more than three weeks since it was repaired for the same fault, so this was, of course, bad news at the beginning of the day.

The technicians normally come once a week to this area if they have got enough jobs to justify the trip from the town of Almeria about ninety kilometres from where we live.

Now it is only a matter of calling them and hoping for the best.

The positive thing is that the wind, which has been blowing all night, has stopped and that we have another sunny day ahead of us.

One of the fist things I do in the morning is to switch on a carousel with a hundred CD's, which throughout the day will provide us with soft background music from a number of loudspeakers spread all over the house and terraces.

My wife is not always as happy as I am to have this music on, particularly when Maria Callas is giving it her best, and her mood is not prepared for it.

Mind you, she has nothing against Maria Callas but the timing must be right.

I press the remote control which, if I do not choose a particular CD, will automatically begin with Pavarotti's beautiful voice, but there is no response.

After having read the instructions for use and tried all the tricks at hand, I had to give in and give up, as there was nothing I could do.

Unbelievable, what kind of statistics would tell you that something like this could happen on the same day.

Like winning in the lottery I believe.

This was definitely not our day and we felt far from winning in the lottery.

The CD player which now has served us for two years has been put aside to be brought to the repair shop for these types of instruments.

Now it remains to be seen if they can repair it at all, or if a new one will have to be bought on a later visit to Gibraltar.

I have not seen them for sale anywhere in Spain.

Black on white   Jan Arnt 2017

Favorite Dream

I have heard that it is very important to have dreams when sleeping. Why that should be I don't know. Everybody dreams it is said, even if one at times doesn't remember the content of one's dreams. There have been periods in my life when I have slept very little, an average maybe 4 hours a night. Normally I would say that a good night for me in this respect would be about five hours.

As my wife is a heavy sleeper, this means that I am awake about three hours more than her every night. So what do I do about it?

At more difficult times of my life I tried to write instead of just lying in bed doing nothing.

That helped me get through, as reading at night never gave me pleasure.

I suppose most of us have some favourite dreams and some we hate.

For me the type of dream that gives me a nightmare is the one that always leaves me short of time to fulfil something.

The dreams may be very different, but the theme is that I always seem to be delayed. Either I cannot find the right way to somewhere I should be at a certain time, or I am being held up by the most incredible situations occurring.

It always ends by waking up, breathing heavily and sweating.

My favourite dream is really wonderful. It has indirectly to do with Newton and the force of gravity.

Imagine, by pure strength of will I lean slowly backwards and find myself floating in the air.

I can then, with the most incredible good feeling, control a kind of flight, either indoors or out in the open.

The flight is controlled by minor, relaxed movements. Never is there any fear that I shall fall down, as I have always landed safely back on my feet.

This type of dream, when it happens, almost always takes place late in my sleep.

The general problem is that I may have only one of my favourite dreams for every three to five of the other ones.

Last night however, something very rare happened, I had one of each.

The first one took place on a golf course which scarily had any fairways and greens, but looked more like a wood.

We were a flight of four fighting our way through the course while the next flight was crowding in from behind. I do not know why we did not let them pass like we normally would.

It was muddy and vet and I hit it the ground more than the ball. To top it off, I lost several balls.

To make a long story short, I think we also lost our way on one hole, ending up on another.

We never finished the round, and when I woke up sweating, the last thing I remember was that I was missing a four iron which I must have lost during the struggle.

Half dozing for the next few hours I went into the wonderful feeling described above.

It all happened indoors, like on a covered tennis court. There was one person watching, which I cannot remember ever having happened before.

This gave an extra good feeling, because I then had a witness to my doing the impossible.

After having been floating around the room for quite a while, I landed safely, after which I gently woke up.

To my daughter Anne-Marie on her 20th birthday:

The best thing about life is that it`s yours.
The most difficult can be to acknowledge it,
to take the initiative and do something about it.
GM

Concience

I suppose conscience is something we are all concerned about. Whether it be good conscience or bad, it will always be there as part of our daily life. Then there is something about suppressing a bad conscience and the pleasant feeling one gets from a good one.

It may have to do with important things or just silly little things, but it is always on our conscience.

Not much harm has been done to houses or trees during the very heavy winds we have had lately, and apart from a few heavy flowerpots tilting but not breaking, just one big one on the upper terrace with an evergreen bush, was broken into pieces.

In that condition it has been standing, or rather lying up till now.

Strangely enough, it looks as if the bush is still alive. Well, I have had a bad conscience about doing nothing with it until now.

Every day I have been looking at it saying to myself that I have to do something about it, but have not managed to pull myself together to take action.

I had a small but nagging bad conscience which finally left me this morning, as I pulled myself together and bought a new pot.

Pretty big and heavy it is, but now it has been brought up onto the terrace, ready to take the place of the broken one.

The gardener visiting us once a week, on Fridays, will do the replanting tomorrow.

While on the way to buy the new pot, I came to think about the fact that we also for almost a year now, have been talking about getting a hands-free system for our mobile phone, to be used in the car.

Again, it has given me a slightly bad conscience as we never seem to get around to doing anything about it.

Now, there is a new law in Spain totally forbidding any use of the mobile while driving.

This gave me an extra push to do something about it.

So, after having manoeuvred the big pot into the car, I passed the sales office where we once bought our mobile, and with 12,500 pesetas less in my pocket I left the shop having got rid of another tiny bad conscience.

Flying thoughts   Jan Arnt 2017

Bomberos

Moods, good moods and bad moods, we all have them; it's just a matter of how we tackle them. One thing is for sure and that is that no one is free from having his or her moods. It's only a matter of controlling them, or isn't it?

Is it good to be able to control your moods? Personally I don't think it is good to control them too much, although I must admit to thinking that it's one of my greatest weaknesses.

I think one would be much happier if one managed to express one's moods.

Today has been one of these typical days which for one reason or other has turned out somewhat special.

What we did is of no interest and it had nothing to do with our private life, but things didn't work out.

Coming home in the afternoon in gale force wind, we both felt that things were not as they should be.

While I was spending a good hour in the office with the wind hammering and whistling all around, my wife came to tell me that she had seen the "bomberos", the fire engine, driving up the mountain, followed by the Guardia Civil police with their blue lights on.

They passed our house and made their way along the dirt road all the way to the top, almost a thousand meters above sea level. She was very uneasy as the wind was about the strongest we have ever felt, at least since the big fire happened here in August ninety-eight.

She admitted to being very uneasy about the situation and that she felt something was wrong.

Women's intuition is never to be underestimated, but on the other hand, when these kinds of intuitions appear after having had what one can call a bad day, one should not necessarily pay too much attention to them.

Easy for me to say, as I myself was also made uneasy by the continued hammering and whistling of the wind.

I have to mention that the day before yesterday one of the residents of our Urbanization arrived from England in his helicopter.

We had seen him flying around both yesterday and today.

It is not very often he is here, but when it happens he normally lands in the car-park of the riding stables at the bottom of the hill.

We had seen him there several times, but the last time we saw him this afternoon he had parked his helicopter on the little closed down airstrip a few kilometres away. Maybe it would be safer there in the strong wind.

From where we live we can see both the riding stables and the little airstrip. A moment ago, just before dawn, we checked both places through our binoculars, without seeing the helicopter.

Was this a sign that something could have happened to him, or had he already taken off to somewhere else? We exchanged a few thoughts about the subject, without reaching a conclusion.

The last thing we saw was the blue light from the Guardia Civil car on the very top of the mountain.

(The next day we found out that the helicopter had been parked on the airstrip throughout the windy night, but in a place where we could not see it.

The reason why the "bomberos" and the Guardia Civil were on the mountain we never found out).

 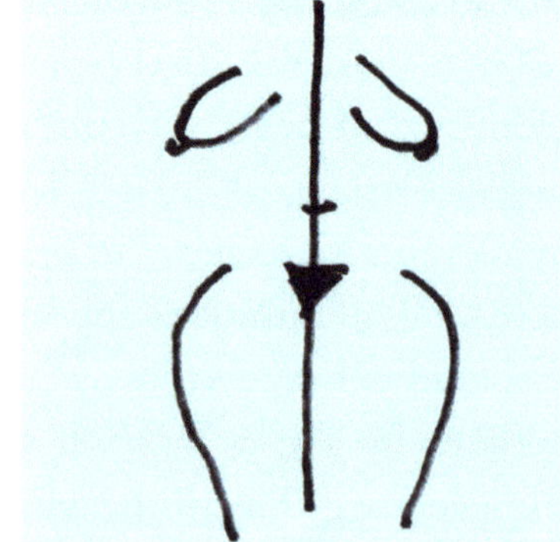

Man's thoughts   Jan Arnt 2017

Physision Control

I went for my yearly check-up in September last year. It was two years since last time, and I must admit I was a little nervous. Having passed sixty I think it is very important to make a complete check-up once a year. Everything turned out to be O.K. apart from the fact that my blood pressure was too high.

Nothing very alarming, but enough for the doctor to want me back within a month to look at the situation and eventually put me on pills.

This is the first time in my life I have had such information, so needless to say it made me a little shaky.

I have never been on special pills before and as I did not fancy the idea too much I asked my wife if there was anything I could do in the meantime to lower the pressure.

I think it is well known to everyone that reducing weight is an important factor as well as sticking to a diet suitable for the purpose.

Nothing else for it but to take the bull by the horn, the challenge was clear. Losing weight I thought meant just to eat less and that could not be very difficult.

But then, when you have a wife who is a very good cook and you are really fond of her cooking, it is easier said than done.

One thing is worth mentioning about my wife's cooking and that is that she follows her cook book very closely.

As we are only two people in our household, and most of the dishes in her books are meant for four, this is what she cooks for. I have, of course, tried to tell her that it should be possible to halve the various ingredients, but in vain.

I think doing that would affect her concentration or otherwise destroy the pleasant time we normally have together in the kitchen while she is cooking.

It may be easy to understand who has the greater part of the portions, when I tell you that my wife weighs only 54 kilos and, that I was brought up in a decent home where I learned to always finish what was on my plate.

We discussed the matter and as part of the diet we decided to go for more fish and only eat meat once a week.

Coffee with milk was abandoned by me from that day on, together with a lot of other smaller but good things.

Being consistent it took me less than four weeks to go from eighty-eight and a half to eighty-three and a half kilos without really suffering.

My next meeting with the doctor proved that my efforts had been successful.

The blood pressure was back to an acceptable level and I was extremely happy.

Now it was only a matter of continuing, something that has proven to be a little more complicated then I thought, with all the temptations around.

After having spent Christmas and New Year's not having kept up with our diet, but still having had quite a few rounds of golf, I hoped that things would be all right.

However, when I got on the scales this morning and saw the figure eighty-five, I took it as a reminder that things do not come by themselves. You have to fight for them all the time.

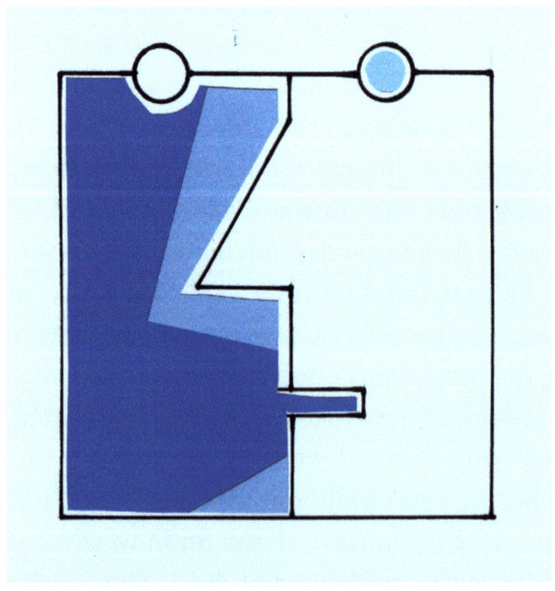

Ambiguous thoughts   *Jan Arnt 2017*

Stopping smoking

It definitely must have happened to hundreds of millions of people, and It probably happens to many millions every day. Well, a lot of things happen to a lot of people every day, but what I have in mind are all those people who wake up in the morning saying to themselves they will quit smoking.

Why I say that it must happen to many millions every day and that it continues to be so many is, of course, due to the fact that although their intention is to quit, unfortunately only a tiny percentage manage to do so.

I suppose that the idea to stop does not happen over night, it is an ongoing process, but one day they will take action and say: today is the day I will quit smoking.

In my business I have supported endless attempts by employees to stop, and paid for all kinds of courses and stop smoking campaigns.

Normally the deal was that half the cost of such courses would be paid back by those joining the, if they started smoking again less than six months after they stopped.

I never let anybody pay back their part, but if I had done so, the company would have saved at least half of the total cost.

The hidden cost in form of lost performance during the campaigns, was never mentioned.

Don't misunderstand me, I am all for smokers trying to quit this horrible habit which is not only very dangerous for one's health but also causes terrible discomfort for the non-smokers living close to them.

My own sad experience, however, shows little hope for us non-smokers of breathing in fresh air, unless we distance ourselves from the smokers.

Although most smokers these days are paying attention to non-smokers, there are still many who claim that they are in their full right to smoke wherever they want to.

Many do not care, either they say it is too late to quit anyway, or they have got the idea that smoking will only destroy someone else, not them, because in their family people have been smoking for generations and none have died from it.

To a certain extent I think it is only fair that people be able to decide about their own situations, even after hearing the costs involved in trying to cure illnesses caused by smoking.

The older I get, the more egoistic I become, and the less I think about people's health in this respect. I personally find the smell that smokers spread around them, both from themselves and from their "clouds" very bad. Not that we non-smokers don't smell, but it is of a different kind.

When you are in love with someone who smokes and you are a non-smoker, it really becomes a challenge.

Unfortunately my wife is a smoker, but as such I must say that she is making her utmost effort not to make my life unpleasant. Nevertheless, I know that she would love to quit so when she this morning finally came with the famous words, I greeted them with enthusiasm. She is not someone who makes such statements often, so I listened very carefully.

The day went well until we later in the afternoon were sitting on the sofa looking at the news.

There it was again this unmistakable bad smell, but this time from having had only one cigarette all day.

Time will show if she joins the millions and millions of people who quit smoking every day.

Styrke

Når det handler om styrke, vi tenker på stål-
men fremstå det kan som den mykeste ål.

Med varme kan mangt få andre former og
derved skapes det nye normer.
GM

Tennis Tournament

Coincidences happen all the time. They happen more often than I think should be possible, seen from a statistical point of view. What about this situation as an example. Has it never happened to you that you have called someone, just to find out that the person you have called at the same moment was lifting the receiver to call you?

Often it is, of course, just something that the person you have called says to please you. But try turning it around and see if it hasn't happened to you that you have received a call from someone at the same moment you were about to call that person.

At least it has happened quite a few times to me.

I think we all know that probabilities are part of statistics.

What then about this example which I am sure that many of us have experienced.

You travel to a city in a foreign country, a city you don't visit too often, let's say Paris. Walking down the main streets you encounter your neighbour, or a person you know from your home town.

How is that possible seen from a statistical point of view? Without going into details I think this is where the probabilities come in.

As our CD player is in for repairs, and we like to have some music on while having dinner, I turned on our local TV-channel.

This is one of the twenty-two channels on our local cable television system, giving information in still pictures about the place where we live and the events taking place. As this channel normally also plays lovely music I thought it was a good idea to put it on.

Due to power-cuts it happens every now and then that this channel, which is controlled by a computer program, stops. What then happens is that it has to be manually reset to continue.

I have very seldom seen it stop on a specific picture; normally when that happens it shows a meaningless image.

In the middle of our meal, the music stopped and the picture of the participants in the latest local tennis tournament froze.

This in itself I must say we found very strange as we didn't notice any power-cut, and while we were still looking at each other in surprise, the telephone rang.

My wife answered it and started speaking French, her mother tongue.

As I do not speak French I understood very little, apart from who had called, as she mentioned her name.

It was the daughter of some very good friends of hers from years ago, long before I met her. They used to have a house in this area, but have long since left.

Their daughter calls us about once a year as she is very fond of my wife and apart from that loves this place.

You may not immediately see the coincidence here, but for us it was very special when the music stopped, as if it had been ordered to, only seconds before the telephone rang.

With my wife on the phone I would in any case have had to stop the music.

The chief thought   Jan Arnt 2017

Hyundai Coupe

The day has been full of events, among them one which doesn't happen too often. It was the day when we ordered a new car. For a long time we have been planning to get a four wheel drive car. The place where we live, about half an hour's drive from the Mediterranean and four hundred meters above Sea level with plenty of possibilities to make trips in the mountains behind us, providing you have a car of this type, triggered the idea already quite some time ago. Last summer we saw the first written presentation of the Hyundai Santa Fe, at that time still to come. As my wife already has a Hyundai Coupe and we are very satisfied with both the car and the excellent local service, we decided to wait for it to come on the market.

As we were picking up the drawings for our new project of twenty town-houses from the architect, the mobile rang, and the Hyundai dealer in the nearby little town called Cuevas de Almanzora was on the line.

He could proudly tell us that he the same morning had received the very first sample of the Santa Fe model, and asked if we would like to see it.

As the architect's office is half-way to the dealer, we decided immediately to have a look.

Half an hour after having seen it, we left the shop having signed for the purchase of a silver coloured hundred and seventy horsepower four wheel drive Santa Fe, which probably will be delivered in February.

We were also very happy with the first layout of the project for the new houses which we had picked up at the architect's, so all in all this should have turned out to be a good day.

But, as my wife is in the process of quitting smoking and feels very low, and as I have a lot of thoughts tumbling around in my head, I could not be of great support to her.

The well-advanced announced eclipse was going to take place a little before nine o'clock in the evening, and I had put up the telescope to be able to have a closer look at it.

We had just finished our meal when I could see the first shadow on the moon.

At the same time my youngest daughter called to say that she had been to visit the grave of Nicoline, her two-year-older sister who died from cancer eleven years ago at the age of twenty-seven.

Placed on the grave she already had found a few candles.

She was the one to remind me about the coincidence between Nicoline's birthday and the eclipse taking place.

I took a last look through the telescope just as the moon was almost totally covered by the earth, and felt a few tears running slowly down my cheeks.

Mass Escape　　　　　*Jan Arnt 2017*

Rebajas

In Spain they call them "rebajas". In English I suppose they are called sales. They mostly take place at the beginning of the New Year and after the summer holidays. This may vary from country to country but it is amazing to see how we, the customers, are being manipulated. I don't necessarily mean this in a negative way, as I suppose this is part of the pattern which makes the big commercial wheel turn.

One interesting point however, is that if you visit certain shops and stores, you will find that products or qualities they normally don't stock, are displayed during the sales.

In other words I have got the feeling that this isn't only the time when existing stocks are sold out to make place for new ones, but also the time when products specially produced for the "rebajas" are brought in for sale. Nevertheless, this is quite o.k. with me, as I normally only purchase something when I am in need of it, and don't delay a purchase in order to get a cheaper bargain.

When I, at the beginning of November last year found myself four to five kilos lighter than the month before and as I, at least as I see it today, intend to stay like this if possible, it also meant that I could no longer wear my old trousers, as I found them completely unsuitable.

As we live in the countryside with only three smaller towns in the neighbourhood, I have found one clothing store which suits me in the city of Almeria, one hour's drive from home.

I felt very happy after one day having bought four pairs of trousers, two for leisure wear and two which were a bit more elegant.

Needless to say, as there were no "rebajas"on they were all at full price.

As you can imagine, I felt great when I took all my old trousers and hung them in the basement. You can never know what will happen.

This took place a couple of months ago, and although I, through Christmas, had some difficulties maintaining my weight, I am now back on the right track.

Today was the day when we had to do some other errands in Almeria, so when my wife was doing something else I went to my shop to buy some more trousers.

My wife is much more aware than me about the "rebajas", and as this was the right time for them she urged me to make the most of the opportunity.

When I saw that almost everything in the shop was for sale at half price I really thought I had to go for it.

The shop was of course pretty crowded which meant there was little help to be had.

Nevertheless, I went on as best I could, and ended up with three new pairs of the slightly more elegant type and four pairs for leisure. On top of it all, I could not resist a blue Yves Saint Laurent shirt, also at half price.

Back home, happy and in good spirits, I put them on one by one for my wife to adjust the length. She marked the length with pins so we can later take them to our seamstress in Turre.

As the seamstress is the wife of the postman, whose office is a hole in the wall and open only two hours a day, it is very convenient to both deliver and collect jobs like this there. If delivered directly to the seamstress, my wife will understandably have to spend almost half an hour having, for the sake of politeness, to listen to the latest gossip.

I started with the three more elegant ones which I had also tried on in the shop. A few centimetres shorter and they will be superb.

The first of the four leisure ones, which I had also tried on in the shop, also needs to be shortened a couple of centimetres to be perfect. The next three pairs, however, which I had not tried on as I thought they were the same as the first ones, turned out to have the same size, no mistake there, but they had a different type of front which actually made them one size too small.

Now, could this be an incentive to reduce a kilo or two more?

Anyway, I decided not to try and exchange them. Keeping them could give me the little extra motivation needed in order to fit into them, which would not do me any harm.

Reflexology

I suppose everyone has experienced a bad back sometime in their lives. So have I, but maybe a little more than the average person. I have also had some nasty falls on skies and a few other self-inflicted injuries, which did not help. Already when I was in the middle of my twenties I had x-rays taken of my back which showed that, the discs between my vertebrae, were in pretty bad shape.

Playing golf I don't think is a problem if you manage to play without using too much force, which you are not supposed to in any case, use too much force that is.

But unfortunately, since my wife and I went to the "David Leadbetter Golf Academy" in the autumn of ninety-nine, I have been struggling with my game.

I use much too much force which is directly affecting my back.

To play in a more relaxed manner is easier said than done, but I am working at it.

I have learned to live with my back problem, but have also tried to do something about it.

In our nearby little town of Garrucha a woman called Lillian runs a little perfumery. She is originally from Czechoslovakia, but has lived here for quite a few years.

In the basement of her shop she has all the facilities needed for doing massages. I think she is a specialist in zone therapy, but as I have now used her on an off for for quite some time for back massage, I think she is just as qualified for that.

If I had only been able to go to her last autumn when I felt it was needed, I would probably have been much better off with my back than I am.

Unfortunately for her, while rescuing her little daughter from falling down some stairs she stumbled, fell and broke both legs. Fortunately everything was all right with her daughter, but she herself was sent to hospital in great pain.

The damage was very severe and she suffered for a long time.

Of course I felt sorry for her when I heard about it one day when I was passing by to make an appointment for a round of massages, but I must admit I also felt a little sorry for myself being left with little chance to get rid of my backache.

She was back in the shop just before Christmas, but could hardly walk and was far from fit to do massages.

However, today was the day when she was able to start again and I was her first customer.

I will never understand how this woman, probably in her early thirties, and with a slim figure and seemingly without any special muscles, can have such strength. Normally I don't cry from pain in front of women, but when I'm on her massage table I at times have to tell her to be a bit more gentle to avoid doing so.

Well, I have now booked a few more sessions.

Green production   Jan Arnt 2017

"Villages"

"Tutto il mondo è un paese", is a saying I heard for the first time when I went to school in Italy in the late fifties. What it means when translated directly is that "the whole world is one country", or in other words; more or less, wherever in the world you go you will find that things are very much alike. The comparison becomes easier if you stick to <u>villages.</u> as I have done below.

You have, of course, got different races and cultures, but if you break it down into individuals I believe you will at least find the same pattern of differences in behaviour, politics etc.

This will most likely not apply where the village is inhabited by people who are attracted to the place because of its social status, as people would then be more alike.

Principally I would say that there are two different kinds of communities.

One is where people have lived for generations, and still are.

New generations take over from the old, but the pattern continues.

Some families do not speak to each other for reasons not necessarily related to big disagreements, but for incidents which happened between the families in earlier generations.

It simply takes all kinds to make up a society regardless of size. "The whole world is one village".

Then you have the other kind representing more recently established communities or villages.

An example of this could be a place in southern Europe which attracts people who want to spend the latter part of their lives in the sun, or the younger ones who want to spend their holidays there.

Such places will, of course, not have any traditions to lean upon, but the pattern of socializing would be pretty much the same I think. Very soon you will see that certain people get on well together, forming groups and tending to be happy.

You will find the ones that most of the community dislikes, and you will find those who are trying to bridge the gap between the two.

Depending on the age of such communities you will still, as time goes by, see that certain people for whatever reasons do not find themselves at ease, and will leave, opening up for others to come in.

"The whole world is one village".

Today we were invited to a party by some people we have known for a long time and who live in a neighbouring development.

They are some of the few that a couple of times a year will try to gather a group of around thirty for such events.

On this specific occasion they used a catering firm and we were served a great variety of food and wine.

I guess we probably knew about a third of the guests, but we were also introduced to people, who were either friends visiting the hosts, or people from the area whom we had never met before.

Very soon you might have observed, if you were there, that we were all putting our heads together with the ones we normally have contact with, although we tried to make a point of getting in contact with the ones we didn't know.

At one point I was asking a British couple whom I had never seen before if they were visiting the place or if they were living there. They told me they had bought a house in the community about four years ago, which they had renovated.

To my next question if they knew many of the other guests, the answer was, only a few.

They also told me that they knew very few people in the community, even after having spent four years there.

However, they seemed to be quite happy, friends or no friends.

A good thing about us humans is that we are not all alike, but still,"the whole world is one village".

La Envia

Waking up to a very crisp but beautiful morning, we decided to play golf.

Due to a lack of golf courses in our vicinity we have now for more than five years been members of a club about one hour's drive farther down the coast. After having stopped in our local village some 6 kilometres down towards the coast for a "tostada" and for my wife to buy her Spanish newspaper, we enter the motorway and she starts reading.

She will tell me about highlights that she finds interesting and we will exchange opinions about them. Most of the stories will be known to us already from watching both international and local television, but doing it this way shortens the drive.

As the first stretch of the motorway brings us through some mountains, we cannot see the snow on top of Sierra Nevada the way we can from our own house on clear days.

From where we are it takes us about twenty-five minutes before we, far away to our right, again can see the white snow covering the mountaintops.

To our left we can also see Cabo de Gata, the point of the Iberian Peninsula sticking out into the Meditteranean sea in the South Eastern part of Spain.

I suppose that it is logical for all ships to pass this point rather close to the shore, whether they are coming from the inner Mediterranean on their way to Gibraltar and the Atlantic, or vice versa.

Although it's Saturday, I can see five or six big tankers, cargo and container ships, all in a row far away on the horizon. They must surely have a distance between them of quite a few kilometres.

Thinking about it, I always see them whenever I drive along this stretch. I must add that they are so far away that they may only be seen if you are really looking for them.

That gets me thinking about the enormous amount of goods being transported by sea.

I suppose at least a hundred huge ships must pass this stretch every week.

Of course, if you take all the countries around the Mediterranean and add to it all the goods being transported to and from the countries in the far east through the Suez Canal, it would not surprise me if this is one of the busiest shipping routes in the world.

On our way back, after a lovely day of golf in beautiful sunshine, I counted another six of these huge ships, making me think that if this is normal traffic, we are not talking about a hundred, but about several hundred ships passing every week.

Could the average price for each of these ships be around a hundred million dollars? That would make more than half a billion for just the ones I could see.

Not strange that one at times feels small in such a big world.

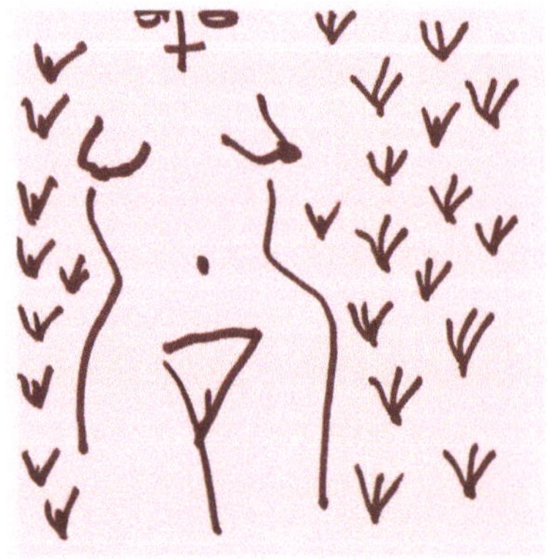

Happy thoughts   Jan Arnt 2017

Lucainena

We have passed the place hundreds of times on the motorway.

The main village of Nijar is situated in a valley between two mountains, not even five kilometres from where we pass. I cannot remember how many times we have said that one day we will have a closer look at it.

People we know have told us that in another very nice village above this one, there is a very good restaurant which is worth a lunch visit.

We have always believed that the village they were talking about is the one we can see above Nijar. It looks smaller but as far as we can judge, it is beautifully situated in the surrounding landscape, and surely must have a breathtaking view down to Cabo de Gata. That is of course, if you don't mind the huge amount of plastic greenhouses that cover most of the flatland in the valley.

After a lazy morning we decided to make an excursion and agreed that the time had come to pay a visit to the village in question.

Our intention was not to have lunch there, but simply have a look around.

My wife remembered that the name of the village we were looking for was Lucainena, so immediately upon reaching Nijar, which in itself we thought was of minor interest, we started looking for the road to Lucainena.

Passing through a few narrow streets we saw the sign, and followed it to the right.

As mentioned we thought that Lucainena was the village that we could see higher up in the valley, and expected to be there within a few minutes.

The road we were on was obviously a very old one. Rather narrow, still with tarmac, though having undergone a lot of repairs. Strangely enough the road was not going up the valley but rather around the mountain to the right of Nijar.

At first we thought it was a matter of just driving around the mountaintop and thereby reaching it, but we soon found out that the village we thought was Lucainena was another one.

As there had been no other exit, we knew we were on the right road.

The landscape had very little vegetation, only the characteristic small bushes. The road took us higher and higher up the mountain, and the slopes down from the road became steeper and steeper. Even if I was driving very slowly, I could see that my wife was not at ease. Neither of us is happy with heights, but as long as it did not get any worse we would be O.K., I thought.

We must have driven close to ten kilometres we reached the highest point of the road. The top of the mountain I estimated to be around a thousand meters above sea level, almost as high as the mountains behind our urbanisation.

Going downhill on the other side, the landscape changed dramatically and became greener and more pleasant, with a splendid view across a huge valley, with a new range of mountains on the other side.

This valley we know very well, as we have driven through it several times on our way to Guadix, where we join the motorway going to the western part of Andalucia.

Apart from a few "fincas" scattered around in the valley, there was no sign of the village until we suddenly saw it while going around a bend. It was beautifully situated under an enormously steep and rocky mountain.

As we approached it we saw plenty of almond trees in blossom and quite a bit of farmed land.

The sign saying Lucainena de las Torres, told us that we had finally reached our village, which instead of being maybe a kilometre or two from Nijar, was almost exactly twenty kilometres away, and on the other side of the mountain.

Driving into the village we soon saw the sign of Venta el Museo, being the recommended restaurant.

As mentioned earlier we had no intention of having lunch, so after a look at the place which seemed nice and full of people, we made a stroll around the lovely village.

We then continued along the road another five kilometres to where it meets the main road, on which it only took us less than half an hour to reach home.

The fire

Last time it happened was during the fire in August ninety-nine. A huge part of the mountain was on fire, but fortunately our village centre just escaped it. Most of the residential area, however, suffered from the fire, leaving most of the houses undamaged, but a few totally destroyed. The fire started about ten kilometres away and lasted for three days. They say that the fire was deliberately started, but so far no one has been arrested. For almost two days the police evacuated everyone and sealed off the whole community.

As my wife is an agent for a British insurance company which covered some of the damaged houses, she was for weeks afterwards involved in sorting out the claims and dealing with the company.

What happened the day after we returned was that a TV team came to have a closer look at the damages. No one knew they would come, they just showed up when we were in a burned-out house with some representatives from the insurance company.

All of a sudden my wife found herself in front of the camera, being interviewed about the place and the fire.

When you are not used to these kinds of performances you could easily end up saying something you will regret, or simply become paralysed.

No such thing, she put on a very good performance, actually one would have thought that she was used to these kinds of events.

Only when I came to think about the fact that she in her younger days used to be a professional model, did I understand that she was, after all, used to being in the limelight.

The mobile rang just after we, this morning, had finished a meeting in a nearby village. It was our sales office calling to say that they had a visit by a woman producer and her cameraman. She spoke to them and arranged for a meeting at our much-frequented coffee bar down at the beach, half an hour later.

It was easy to recognize them when they arrived, as he was carrying his big video camera. They were representing a new digital TV station in Barcelona with fourteen channels.

They were working for one of these, which programs mostly focused on travel.

The woman producer had read an article in El Pais about our village, had been up there this morning and taken shots all over the place.

Now was the time to have an interview with someone who could tell its story. It should only last a few minutes, but was essential for the reportage.

Minutes later it was agreed to make the interview there and then.

They suggested we find a palm or something green as background for the shooting.

Just around the corner we found a little square with a huge cactus and some bushes well situated as background. The setting was perfect they thought.

Out of a bag came the microphone which was plugged into the camera, and so my wife found herself in front of it again, being interviewed and telling them the history of our village, why the architecture was a combination of Moorish and Andalucian, and much more.

Standing within hearing distance I was very impressed by her performance.

I understood most of what she was saying, although my Spanish is rusty. Hers on the other hand is fluent, as she has been living here for almost thirty years.

To be repeated any time.

Organic thoughts   *Jan Arnt 2017*

Ford Fiesta

On our way to the notary we were driving our thirteen year old Ford Fiesta, as the Hyundai Coupe is in the auto repair shop for a few days, for reasons I will tell you later. Although the Fiesta is old, it has not driven more than around sixty thousand kilometres, and works quite well.

In the middle of a wide bend I saw a lorry coming towards me, suddenly cross the white line in the middle of the road and continuing into my lane. My wife was looking through the mail, which we had just collected at the post office, so she was not aware of anything.

I instinctively turned to the right and missed the lorry by less than a meter. In a split second I saw that it was the local water lorry, the one that collects drinking water from the mountain.

As we meet him regularly on our local road, I have for a long time been very irritated about the way he seems to believe that he owns the road, never dreaming of letting anyone overtake him.

Can you imagine the feeling one gets from being behind him on our narrow local road, when he has just filled the tank and moves at about twenty kilometres an hour?

My wife, of course, felt the sideways movement, so I had to tell her what almost happened. She reminded me that this was the third time in less than a month which had almost ended in disaster while driving.

In the more than forty years that I have been driving, I have never, nor has she in her time of driving, been involved in incidents which have left more than a few scratches.

The first of these three narrow escapes happened when we, two days before Christmas Eve, were driving on the motorway towards Arcos de la Frontera in the western part of Andalucia.

It was raining heavily and as I am always thinking about the possibility of water planing, I was taking it easy. It did not seem to bother most of the Spaniards though, as plenty of cars were overtaking us at speeds of up to at least a hundred and sixty.

There is one very dangerous bend on the motor way just outside Malaga, which is very well signposted both for its danger and to reduce speed.

My speed must have been around eighty in the right hand lane, when I was going through the bend. For a split second I saw, in the mirror, a car just beside my left rear wing make a three hundred and sixty degree turn on his wheels, before it felt as if something hit us. As I was slowly braking, my wife asked if we had driven over something on the road. While still braking, I saw again in the mirror, the other car take another complete turn, smash into the cement barrier of the motorway before jumping back into the middle of the two lanes.

I stopped at the side of the road a few hundred meters farther along, and saw plenty of cars coming, braking and passing the damaged one. I also saw people trying to organize the traffic.

We went out to have a look at our car. The most incredible thing had happened. At the end of its first complete turn, the front of the other car had just touched the left rear end of our car, just making a very small dent and leaving some of its blue paint on top of the red.

Shaken by the thought of what could have happened if he had been only half a meter farther ahead when he water-planed, we got back in the car and continued our trip.

There is something about being "at the wrong place at the wrong time". It was not our turn this time, but closer it is impossible to get.

Back home for New Year's Eve and the start of two thousand and one.

On one of the first days of the New Year we had to go to Almeria. On the motorway on what was a beautiful sunny day, I slowly got closer and closer to a huge trailer. They normally have a speed of about a hundred and so had he, while I was driving at about a hundred and thirty. I was signalling to overtake him when I saw him cross over into the left lane, something I found very strange as he had no cars in front of him.

I slowed down, only to see that he had turned to the right again, smashing the side of his trailer into the metal rail, which we could see moving and making sparks fly everywhere. He then slowly got back into the right lane again. I took my time in overtaking him, only to see that he had a big map in front of him and that the lorry came from Belgium.

This time nothing happened, but what if we had been beside him when he made his first manoeuvre?

Twice our Hyundai Coupe has been scratched while parked in a garage in Almeria, so now you understand why it's in for repairs and we are driving the old Fiesta.

Colourful thoughts   *Jan Arnt 2017*

Birthday

This was one of the few days on which we had no appointments, apart from our daily visit to the building site. We do that more or less every day to see how the project of eight town houses is getting on. The builder shows us around and we discuss all kinds of matters related to the project. With no other appointments we therefore decided to make it a day of shopping.

First we went to collect the CD player, which has now been in the workshop about two weeks.

We have had very good experience with the repair shop, as they have earlier mended two TV sets and an amplifier for us. Well, it was not ready yet, as they had to get a new laser pick-up from the supplier. It had been ordered and they expected to get it within a week. I must admit I was happy as, after all, they would be able to repair it. Our next mission was to collect some pictures, which had been framed. They should have been finished already last Friday, but for reasons I did not understand when she obviously tried to explain it to me, they would not be ready until this afternoon. Not too bad, after all, only a few days delay.

I am not a big spender on myself when it comes to clothes and other personal things. As an example, for the last fifteen to twenty years I have only worn watches which I either got as Christmas presents from suppliers, or watches that our company had bought to give away to special customers.

I must admit, however, that I once, about thirty years ago, bought a beautiful and not inexpensive Rado watch, during one of my visits to Switzerland. I still have it, but the chain which is an integrated part of the watch, was worn out after about ten year's use, and beyond repair.

My son in law, being the marketing manager of our company, must have registered what kind of watch I am wearing. For my sixtieth birthday he arranged for the company to buy me a lovely Omega.

My wife must have registered the same, for she also gave me a lovely Swiss watch, but this one, contrary to the sporty Omega only to be worn on special occasions.

Also when it comes to sunglasses I have only bought the cheapest models when I felt I needed them.

Apart from once, about thirty years ago, when I was heading the Norwegian clay pigeon shooting team at an international competition in Montecatini in Italy. I bought a pair of original Ray Bans making the excuse that I needed them for shooting. I have had them until now, and since I started living in Spain have only worn this one pair. Now, however, after having repaired them several times, they are falling apart completely.

Both my wife and I wear glasses, both for reading and watching TV, and the shop we normally use for glasses have just moved across the street into new and more modern premises.

While passing it I decided to buy myself a new pair of sunglasses and we went in. Convinced that I could get away with a cheap pair, I started by trying on various ones from a stand.

To cut a long story short, after twenty minutes I came out with a fairly expensive pair of Porsche Design.

A little farther along, Benneton have also moved across the street to new premises, and when my wife saw the sign "rebajas" in the window, it was as if a magnet pulled her in.

Two pairs of trousers, a jumper and a sweater were added to our purchases; before we again hit the road and made a trip to the shop I love the most.

Ferreteria Lopez is the most fantastic shop. If I say they sell everything it's, of course not the truth, but if you went in there with me, you would agree.

All kinds of tools, both electric and manual, screws and nails, paints, toys, machinery and everything for the garden, even plants. Televisions, radios and CD's. Everything for the kitchen including refrigerators, cookers and all kinds of electrical equipment, outdoor furniture, everything for pets, and even clothes; I could go on.

Normally I go there alone to equip my hobby room with all kinds of things I need, but today we went there together. We needed more hangers for her new trousers, and the ones I bought the other day.

We then stopped at the Parque Comercial to buy fish and vegetables, before having a coffee and some water at the coffee shop in the plaza.

We just reached home in time for the Spanish news at three o'clock.

Birdwatcher

We have at least one "bird watcher" in the village. Every now and then I ask him if he has seen anything special or interesting.

As I used to be a keen hunter, I always listen to people with interest in wildlife.

Beside shooting grouse in the season, my first reindeer I shot when I was fourteen.

However, I soon found out that I was no butcher and turned to hunting birds only and limiting myself to that. Hunting birds and shooting clay pigeons became my main hobby for many years, until I took up golf.

Last time I spoke to the "bird watcher" he told me that he now knew where the eagles had their nest.

We usually have a pair of eagles in our mountains, but it is a long time since I have seen them. I must admit that I was impressed that someone had found their nest. He said that the nest was discovered merely by accident by someone from the village having a Sunday walk in the mountains.

He had only told this to the "bird watcher" and to no one else.

I do not think he would have told me where it was, but the way he described it in general terms it could not be more than two or three kilometres up the mountain.

It is crazy at times to hear about people collecting eggs of all kinds. They will do anything to rob a nest if it belongs to a rare type of bird. I am pleased they have heavy fines and even jail sentences for these kinds of people when they are caught.

Well, I suppose most birds have their nests as their home and the place where their little ones see the light of day for the first time. They are not always in trees, and the nest of these particular eagles cannot be in a tree I believe, as there are very few trees in these mountains.

Bird nests on the ground are, of course, more vulnerable than the ones in trees, but again, in nature there are different kinds of enemies. I am sure nature itself has found the best solution for making them survive and generate.

I suppose it is the same for other types of animals than the birds. Many of them also make their nests in the strangest places.

Our Hyundai Coupe is always parked outside our main entrance in front of the garage.

Why not in the garage you may ask.

Well I am afraid there is no space for it in there.

Anyhow, to the right of the garage, a wild palm is growing which, having being watered, has grown quite big for its kind. The last few months it has been full of fruit, which were green at first but have now turned brown.

Today was the day when we were to collect the car from the garage, where it has had some minor scratches fixed.

Off we went to Cuevas de Almanzora in the old Fiesta. Juan was there ready to present us with the bill, as we knew the car was ready after having called him. First he showed us, proudly and with a big smile, the quality of the repairs.

Then his face turned sad as he said there was something he was not so happy about.

As he was on his way to open the bonnet, I thought something serious had happened with the car. With his big smile turned back on, however, he showed us that a nest covered the whole area on top of the battery.

In the middle of it I could count what I thought was about a dozen brown oval-shaped eggs. A closer look told us they were not eggs, but fruit from the palm.

Can you imagine the little mouse or rat sitting somewhere outside the garage in the chilly winter afternoons, waiting for her warm house to appear?

Then when the monsters in it had disappeared, she would find her way from below to her warm and cosy nest.

The only thing we can wonder about is what would have happened the day the little ones had woken up under the bonnet.

I am afraid we saw no other way in which to solve the problem but to clear the battery of the nest, and we can only hope that the little animal will find a more permanent place to raise her family.

Junta de Compensacion

I feel certain that the judicial system in Spain is the same as in the rest of Europe, but my impression is that it is practised in a very different way. When you look at the big ases, as for instance the Mayor Jesus Gill in Marbella, it is impossible to understand how he can still maintain his job after all the years he has been in severe trouble.

I do understand that these kinds of cases are very complex, but according to what you can read about it, it is unbelievable that he is still free and not behind bars. Another thing is that people seem to appreciate him, and wants him to continue as Mayor.

Well, our little Building activity in Cabrera also has its judicial side. During the years I have lived here, I have witnessed quite a few cases which seemed to be totally obvious, but which in the end turned out to go the wrong way, or simply kept going on and on until they seem to evaporate.

People here do not seem to care at all, and honesty is a word which rarely seems to be used or practised. Everything is a matter of how you can twist, bend and delay matters.

Of course, all of this is only my impression and, mind you, we must not forget that this is in Andalucia, with its close to eight million people. Nothing wrong with Andalucia, on the contrary, as it is the place where the sun spends the winter, but if the rest of Spain works like this, I really cannot understand how they can cope.

Today for instance, my wife was called into court as a witness in a criminal case that she has had to make against a person who has written a false contract using her signature.

The contract states that she has let an office, which belongs to a company she manages, to this person. As my wife, at a certain time a couple of years ago, wanted to make use of the office herself, he absolutely refused to move out. She had no choice but to go to court.

The case would have been rather simple we believe, if it was not for the fact that when he was called, he presented this false contract.

The worst thing is that the signature could well be hers, as the same person earlier had access to papers with her signature on them.

As the president of the local "Junta de Compensacion" for five years, she often had to leave behind a couple of blank papers with her signature on them, to be used in emergency cases when she was travelling. The same person then, as a "miembro de delgados" in the "Junta de Compensacion", also had access to the office in which these papers were kept.

If it should turn out that the signature, which when seeing it she admitted was very much like hers, is in fact hers, what then?

The contract in itself, even if it is very clumsily written, allows him to stay in the office.

When she was at the court today, she was not allowed to state her point of view, but simply had to answer questions being asked by the female judge. She was also asked to write her name and a few sentences dictated by the judge.

Present in addition to her and the judge was a secretary, someone representing her lawyer and, of course, the lawyer of the accuser.

As she answered the questions, the judge dictated a resume to the secretary, who typed it on an ordinary typewriter.

In less than half an hour the whole thing was over. Everybody read the resume which they all signed. The secretary made one copy for each participant and that was it.

On what basis the verdict will be made I do not know, but I have a strong feeling that if they find the signature on the contract to be hers, she will lose the case. If that is so, she can certainly appeal, but this will probably take a year or two at least, so most likely in the end he will stay in the office and the case will evaporate.

The snake   Jan Arnt 2017

Fish on the way   Jan Arnt 2017

The Presidents

This is the day when a new page in the history books of the United States is written. George Walter Bush was sworn in as the forty-third American President, with almost the smallest margin that has ever happened. Conservative, claiming he will run the country in a democratic way, he highlights among others, a stronger defence using new technology, more help to the poor, and a strengthening of the educational system.

Indubitably he has a strong opposition against him, something I find quite natural, after President Clinton's eight years in power.

Personally I am a conservative, disliking most, if not all, of the "isms" like Communism, Nationalism, Socialism and all kinds of extremism. All the "ism" people live under the banner of protecting people, but at the end of the day it is more a matter of controlling than protecting, I think.

Of course, right wing Conservatism, which in my eyes also belongs to extremism, is not good either.

But all in all I believe that a Conservative rule gives more progression than a Democratic one.

What a coincidence that the Philippines also got a new Prime Minister today. Mrs. Arroyo took over from "what's his name"? I think it is good that I have forgotten the name, as he apparently has stolen more than sixty million dollars from the state, and can risk a lifetime behind bars if prosecuted and found guilty.

They claim that the process of changeover has happened in a democratic way. Let us therefore hope Mrs. Arroyo will be given a chance to work out some guidelines which will be to the better for these eighty some million people, and that she will be allowed to go through with them.

I wonder, with all the islands that this country consists of, how many ferries and other seagoing vessels they have, to link them together.

I think that far too often we can read about ferry tragedies happening over there, with huge casualties.

Apart from these, and surely many other big things happening in the world today, we witnessed something, which for the ones involved, or at least for the winners, could possible change their lives.

That is at least what they say about being Miss Universe.

Well, we are not talking about that, not even Miss Spain, but simply Miss Almeria. Almeria is a city of about a hundred and seventy thousand inhabitants, nevertheless, the contest must mean a lot to its participants.

A lot of small towns and villages belong to the province of Almeria, and each of them, have of course far in advance selected its beauty to represent them in the Miss Almeria contest.

Arriving at our Golf Club, we were met by a packed car-park, something which is totally unusual even on a Saturday.

On the terrace in front of the clubhouse we saw a team of cameramen representing different newspapers and local TV stations, and surely also some reporters.

Around twenty of the most beautiful girls from the area were dressed up in wine-coloured blazers, with a white banner displaying the name of the place they represented as finalists, running from one shoulder down to the opposite hip.

During the few minutes we were in the middle of this event, before my wife insisted that we were there to play golf, they were put into two rows, one behind the other, cameras flashing.

After we had finished our round, something like four hours later, they were still being photographed, but this time one by one behind the first tee.

I have been around a lot in my life but must admit that I have never seen so many beautiful girls gathered together in one place at the same time.

As usual we sat down to have our beer and "tapas" in the bar before driving home. We were both giggling about how my neck, stiff after playing golf, definitively did not improve during the half hour we were sitting there.

Nature picture

It is possibly the ugliest sight imaginable. From where we stand behind the first tee on this beautiful sunny morning, we get a glimpse of the sea way down there between two mountains. Only if you know the area well are you aware that only half of what you see is the sea, the rest is plastic. The area around El Ejido borders the village of Adra in the west, the mountains in the north, and the towns of Aguadulce and Roquetas in the east.

It contains an enormous amount of plastic-covered land where all kinds of vegetables are grown.

El Ejido they say is one of, if not, the richest area in the whole of Spain, but it must also be one of the least attractive.

The area under plastic must be around forty to fifty kilometres long and at least ten kilometres wide. With the sun and, in later years, a continuously improved watering system, no place in Europe can compete with what they produce here.

Tragically enough this is also the place where immigrants have been, and still are, greatly abused. None-registered workers from Morocco and other places in Africa are working long hours at very low wages.

The Spanish authorities are well aware of the problem, of course, but seem to have difficulties finding a quick solution to the problem. They are registering more and more of the immigrant workers, as I suppose that for the Spaniards themselves it is very unattractive to say the least, to work in such extreme conditions under plastic.

Every now and then you can read in the papers that there are fights and even killings amongst these people.

There will always be some employers who treat them well, but most of the immigrant workers as I understand it, live under very bad conditions.

An event that happened a fortnight ago really got the debate going. It did not happen in Andalucia, but just on its border, in the province of Murcia.

A van with nine immigrant workers and a Spanish driver, including a thirteen year old girl, taking her sick mother's place for the day, collided with a train. Everyone was killed but the girl.

The employer was arrested and will certainly, and for good reasons be in great trouble, as it turned out that they had been very badly treated, and paid an absolute minimum wage.

As long as there are opportunities there will be abuse, but we must also remember that Andalucia is the part of Spain with the greatest percentage of illiterates. As a result of that I suppose many of the worst abusers are land-owners with no experience of being responsible for other people, with limited education, and having started cultivating their land now see it turning into big business.

It is strange to think about the fact that just on the outskirts of this huge area, you have quite a few big tourist resorts, which attract people from all over Europe. Everyone coming there must drive through this sea of plastic, but most probably they don't for a second imagine the many tragedies that a lot of people suffer here.

Now it is our time to tee off and enjoy the lovely golf course situated between the mountains.

Blue thoughts Jan Arnt 2017

Speeding ticket

Spain has, like most modern countries, a bureaucracy which is very difficult to understand for a foreigner, or at least for me. I have made a few observations, however, about a couple of things which seem to work differently from and, in my opinion, better than they do in Norway, where I have lived most of my life.

The first has to do with the traffic police and the second with taxes. So far, having driven more than a hundred thousand kilometres in this country, I have only had good experiences with the police.

Twice I have been caught speeding and twice I have been stopped to have my papers checked.

The second speeding ticket I got when I was driving on the motorway from Alicante airport. My wife had picked me up in her first Hyundai Coupe, a very sporty car, which she had received during the weeks I had been away.

Cruising at a speed of around a hundred and twenty or thirty everything went well, but on a long stretch I made a little test and just passed a hundred and fifty. We overtook some cars, of course, but what none of us knew at the time was that the police had cars specially equipped with cameras. All of a sudden I saw a police car several hundred meters in front of me, which made me slow down to a hundred and twenty which is the limit here.

The blue lights came on, and as he slowly started braking, I did as well, until we came to a full stop.

One of the Guardia Civil came up to us, and from what happened next, I thought he could see we were not Spanish.

For this reason I think, he turned to English and said: "You be driving too fat". At the same time I noticed in the mirror that a little white car had stopped as well. Behind its windscreen I could see the camera.

The policeman asked for my driving licence, which I gave him, and while studying it he told me that we had been driving at a hundred and forty-two kilometres per hour.

What could I say?

So far my wife had said nothing, but when he told me that I had to pay the fine of twenty-five thousand pesetas on the spot, she came to the rescue.

She showed him her Spanish "residencia", and explained in fluent Spanish where we lived.

After hearing this, the fine, which had been reduced to twenty thousand, could be paid when we received the bill in the post.

He was very nice and told us that if the picture, which would accompany the bill was not clear enough, we could protest.

After two months we were convinced that the bureaucracy had saved us from paying but, almost three months after the event, the bill came. No picture was enclosed, but we did not bother about that and paid it straight away.

In Norway my experience was that the police on the roads would drive exactly at the speed limit and if you were stupid enough to overtake them, however slowly, you would immediately be stopped and fined. My opinion was that they simply pested you, and disrupted the flow of traffic.

In Spain however, my impression is the opposite. There are many police on the roads, but whether they are in cars or on motorbikes, they will, on the motorway, keep to a speed of around a hundred and ten. They expect you to overtake them, and if you do that carefully you are not in trouble.

Quite another thing is that far too many Spaniards drive like mad, and are seen driving at a hundred and eighty or more all the time.

The tax system is something very special and also different but it seems as if the tax people do not pester you the way they do in Norway. Taxes have to be paid, of course, but it seems like everyone, and that also applies to auditors, is prepared to do their utmost to bring them down to an acceptable level. Because of my wife's business we sat in a meeting all morning listening to the specialist's advice on how to minimize the tax of her companies. An acceptable result was reached, before we totally exhausted went to our little bar for some "tapas".

From the pure excitement and success of the morning, we ate far too much and had to settle for just a salad for dinner.

Detour

Due to the damage made late last year by an enormous amount of water pouring down over a short period of time, the front road from Turre to our village, a stretch of about six kilometres, was severely damaged in a few places. The little bridge in the middle of the stretch was almost totally destroyed, and it took about two months before temporary repairs were made.

By temporary repairs I mean that a detour has been made beside the bridge into and through the riverbed, and up onto the other side.

We suppose that they will wait to make a final repair until spring, as more torrential rain can be expected before that.

The Hyundai Coupe does not favour this kind of detour due to all the bumps so we always use the back entrance, which used to be the front entrance while driving this car.

However, the old blue Ford Fiesta does not mind these kind of challenges at all, and as this is a day when we have a lot of different commitments, we take one car each, and I am now driving down the front road in it.

I don't know when it was left in the car, but it must have been my daughter who did it quite a few years ago. I am talking about a cassette containing a lovely piece of music from the play "Much Ado about Nothing", by William Shakespeare.

Since I saw the film, I have often tried to get hold of the video, not least because I would like my wife to enjoy it. So far I have not succeeded, but I am sure that one day I will find it.

What my wife has not seen on the video, we have both seen in real life.

The film, staring Emma Thompson and her husband at the time, Kenneth Branagh, was shot in Greve in Tuscany, which in my opinion is one of the most beautiful places in Italy.

The whole film was shot on an estate called Vignamaggio which, in the last few years, has been turned into the loveliest little Hostal by the owners. That applies to part of the buildings only, as the family still lives in the main house.

The garden with its beautiful well-kept flowerbeds, hedges and cypresses, I think is unique. The cypresses, by the way, are the largest I have ever seen.

On the road around the estate going up to Lamole, the cypresses grow like an enormous hedge on both sides.

The place was all-together a fantastic setting for the film.

The young woman who was the model for Leonardo da Vinci's Mona Lisa used to live in this house, so for that reason alone the place is well known.

One of my old Italian friends has a lovely mansion a little further up the hillside above Vignamaggio, so that is why I have been there several times.

Two years ago my wife and I went there to celebrate his seventieth birthday, an event we never forget.

Around a hundred people from several countries had a lovely lunch and spent the afternoon in the garden in front of his house that day in June, overlooking the most spectacular hillsides of Chianti.

Under the four huge trees in front of his house, the guests were seated in groups of twelve at round tables protected by big parasols. He had put men and women at separate tables, and for me in particular it was a great pleasure to be with his closest friends at the head table in the middle.

All these good memories came to my mind driving down to the beach to have my hair cut, as the lovely music reminded me of our stay at Vignamaggio those few days in June two years ago.

"Say no more ladies, say no more……..".

Danish dynamite   *Jan Arnt 2017*

China

Far, far away, a huge country with much more than one billion people is today starting its New Year. It's going to be the year of the snake. Impossible to say what the year will bring, but let's hope that more trade and use of the internet, the positive side of it, will gradually form a better understanding between them and the rest of the world.

Whatever we do, it must take time, and it will probably take much longer than we think possible.

I will never forget when I first really understood the challenges they would face in that country if they were to advance too quickly.

About twenty years ago I happened to take the train from Hong Kong to Canton in China. I thought the countryside was beautiful. The enormous terracotta coloured fields really appealed to me.

The trip up to the border was interesting, I thought, but not so very special.

However, walking over the bridge, which marks the border between Hong Kong and China, gave me a feeling I will never forget.

I don't remember if we changed trains but, anyway, we had to walk that stretch carrying our own luggage. Don't forget that this was the early days of reformation in China, but they still searched everything we brought with us.

I was there together with a friend, who at that time imported eiderdown to Europe in considerable quantities. Ha had been in China many times before and was considered a "good old friend of China". I was registered as his designer to get a visa, and we were going to Shanghai for a week.

When the train left the station on the Chinese side of the river, I felt like I was going into noman's land. As I said, the nature was beautiful, and the brown and yellow colours of the rather flat land were breathtaking.

I don't remember seeing any cars on the whole trip, apart from when we approached Canton.

A few motorbikes and I think less than a dozen lorries.

The trip, as far as I remember, took about four hours.

But what about tractors, why did we not see any of those, as on one side of the train we could see, almost all the way, enormous cultivated fields.

We were talking about this when I observed something very strange.

Far away out in the field, a blue line all of a sudden appeared for a few seconds, only to disappear again. Then, after a few seconds, it appeared again, and so on. The length of this line must have been about half a kilometre.

We wondered about this for a while, until we understood what it was. Instead of using one ordinary tractor, more than five hundred, men and women, had their daily work taking the place of a mechanized plough.

When we later discussed it with people we met, they confirmed that this was a way to keep people at work on the farmland, like the one we had passed.

Standing side by side in rows of any length, they would in one up and down movement, turn the soil over in the same length.

Such a group would represent a tremendous capacity, but I could not help thinking about how many thousands of people would have been out of work if only one of the really big American tractors had been brought in.

Today is also the day of the new moon and the sacred Hindu Festival is taking place in India. Just this very day they expect more than twenty million Hindus to get forgiveness for their sins.

Altogether they expect that the number of those who participate will exceed the total population of the United States of America.

With so many people gathered at the riverside at one time, it is not strange to hear said that families even tie themselves together with ropes so as not to get away from one another.

Everything that has been created, whether it is humans, animals or things built by humans, has to disappear sometimes.

A rocket has today been sent up to connect with the space station Mir. Its time has come after many years of service. It will apparently be given a little push, so its course will bring it back into the atmosphere of the earth, where it will burn up and only leave fragments, which are planned to fall into the Pacific Ocean.

Prostitution

As long as there are people on earth, there will be prostitution. I think it's legal in Spain as I from the very first time I came here have heard so. You can recognise the brothels by the red light outside, and here you can see them, apart from in the cities, every now and then along the roadside, and very often in isolated places.

I am all for the legalisation of prostitution, because then it should be possible to have it under at least some sort of control but it should, of course, in no way involve anyone but grown-ups.

Most grown-ups understand that making prostitution illegal does not stop the oldest trade in the world, so it's much better to have it out in the open than to have it operating illegally.

It would then also be easier to check if the girls are involved voluntarily or not. In this part of Spain we can often read about places where the police have discovered illegal activity and where foreign girls have been kept against their will.

What happens to the ones organizing this trade when they are caught I know nothing about, but I hope they are severely punished.

Only recently we had a case right outside Vera, a town about 20 minutes from where we live. A local politician was caught, not for having visited the brothel of course, but for having been involved in its organization.

In this case it was discovered that girls were kept there against their will. Every evening after the sun goes down if we, from the terrace of our house, look out over the wide valley, we can see some blue and red lights close to the motorway some 10 kilometres away. Of course, at that distance you cannot see the details, but those are the neon lights announcing a club, one of the kind that offer special services.

When passing it at any time of the day or night you normally see a few cars parked outside.

Not far from our golf club you will find a village called El Parador, it has nothing to do with the famous Spanish hotels but the name is easy to remember. In the Almerian papers, Almeria being the largest city in the area, you will find plenty of advertisements for clubs of all kinds, most of them involving prostitution, and quite a few of them with addresses in El Parador.

This morning we could read that three officers of the Guardia Civil police, and two medical doctors, were jailed for having been heavily involved in the organization of a brothel with more than twenty prostitutes. Apparently all the girls were foreigners, having been lured into the situation.

With promises of a job, they had arrived legally, only to find that their passports and other vital papers were taken away from them, and that they were threatened with being handed over to the police if they did not "co-operate positively". From fear of being thrown out of the country I suppose they chose to co-operate

Quite another thing is, according to the paper, that it has now been proven that I am less intelligent.

As a result of not having had an academic education, I am supposed to have had more problems growing up than many others. I admit having problems understanding the logic in this.

New research in England can tell us that babies being born physically skinny will suffer from being less intelligent, they will learn less and will generally have more problems then babies being born fat.

Well, my mother always said, and I think she meant it, that I was born skinny and that I was very ugly as a baby.

It is a fact that I was born skinny, and that I never became an academic. However, I was not born particularly small or fat.

I never did brag about my intelligence, but in general I feel quite happy with what I have achieved in life so far, and definitely don't suffer from any inferiority complex towards fat people.

I must admit however, that in the article I am referring to, they gave us skinny babies a fair chance to cope with the world's challenges, providing we were given good help and care by our parents and were given special assistance with our school work.

I am sure I would have been given good help with my school work if only I had let anyone help me, but I never did as I scarcely did any homework.

It is interesting to read about oneself at times.

The Architect

This was the day when our architect was going to present the finished drawings of the new project of twenty town houses which, if everything goes according to the plan, we will start building in March or April this year. I was particularly keen to see the plans, as I am leaving for Norway tomorrow.

Something happened to delay the group of architects working with the perspective drawings of the first phase of the project, containing the first eleven houses. They now promise to have them ready on Tuesday next week.

I have never been to Africa, but I can remember that I once won a bet about how many countries the continent consisted of.

Bets were made from around fifteen to about thirty, while I won claiming that it was more than forty. Actually, having checked it afterwards, it is close to sixty.

We have all heard about the ongoing problems in Eritrea, the Hutsus, Tutsis and not least, the number of cruel leaders in some of the countries.

Take Idi Amin as an example, but then he later got what he deserved.

Today they are burying Laurent Kabila, and at the same time his son Joseph will be sworn in as the new leader of the Democratic Republic of Congo. We will probably never get to know why one of his bodyguards shot him, and as far as I know we never got to know what happened to him either. Not that it really matters, but I would think that he, amongst a lot of locals, will be looked upon as a hero.

Joseph Kabila swore to follow the constitution, while the reporter, at the same time told us that they do not have a real constitution in Congo, and that no one knows the new leader's exact age. One thing was clear though, he did his military training in China. He will need to get good support from his neighbours, as I understand he has little support from his own country's military.

I will not even pretend that I understand what is going on down there.

We have long talked about it, and today my wife insisted that I take the medical test to apply for a Spanish driving licence, so off we went to Garrucha with pictures and passport.

Apart from discovering that the sight in my left eye was not as good as in the right, everything went well until he checked my blood pressure.

Twice the doctor did the test, without saying anything, before he changed his instrument and tried for the third time. Shaking his head he said it was two hundred and fifteen over one hundred and ten. This I thought was frightening, as I for the same reason lost five kilos last autumn, and started eating much more fish to bring it back to normal again.

What he wrote in the papers I don't know, but he suggested we go straight to the "urgencia", to ask for pills to reduce it.

We were well received, and after having explained the situation to the doctor, he did a new test.

This time, only half an hour after the first, it showed a hundred and ninety over one hundred. We told him how we for the last few days had enjoyed a lovely smoked leg of lamb, brought back from Norway and that it was very salty. Could that have something to do with it?

Without saying much, he gave me a pill to chew and told his nurse to give me an injection in my bottom.

The next step was to wait for half an hour before doing another test. A hundred and sixty over ninety he uttered with a smile, and said it would keep going down.

Then he told me to stay away from too much salt and eat a lot of fruit and vegetables.

As it was my last day before going to Norway for a fortnight, we ordered a steak tartar in our local restaurant Los Pastores. As a starter my wife ordered a carpaccio de solomillo and I a foie gras. After having ice-cream for dessert, something we normally don't and more than normal red wine, we called it a day.

I promised my wife I would consult my doctor in Oslo as soon as possible after arriving.

Blood pressure

The shock I got from my blood pressure reading yesterday has convinced me to keep my promise to my wife and consult my doctor in Norway, explain the phenomena and ask for his advice. Just crossing the Pyrenee Mountains between Spain and France, after a bit of a bumpy ride up to the cruising level of about thirty thousand feet, I came to think about what happened yesterday in South America.

A DC 3 plane went down and all the about twenty-five passengers and crew were killed, most of them tourists from America and Europe.

Apparently the company involved, flying mostly tourists and giving them an experience for life, are using DC 3's, because these aircraft can fly rather slowly and and a low altitude.

The association leading to the above came to me when we took off from Alicante airport.

On the southern side of the airport building they still keep two wrecks of DC 3's. They have been standing there at least since I landed at the airport for the first time, about 15 years ago.

They are not, however, standing at the exact same place as they did then.

The first time I saw them they were closer to the airport building, but as they have extended it, the two planes have now been moved and are placed a few hundred meters farther south.

Why they are still there one can only wonder.

These wonderful machines were first produced in the thirties, and have always been referred to as the working horses of the sky.

One can ask if the allies would have won the last world war if they had not had these machines.

An enormous amount of them were produced and used, not least during the allied invasion of mainland Europe.

They also pulled a huge amount of gliders over the channel, carrying troops and equipment, even cannons and Jeeps.

It is most fascinating to think about the fact that only a decade before these machines were first designed and produced, Charles Lindbergh in his NX 211 was the first single person to cross the Atlantic Ocean in a plane.

That took place on the twentieth and twenty-first of May in 1922, when he was only twenty years old.

I wonder what he felt when he, after thirty-three and a half hours, almost collapsing with tiredness, managed to land at Le Bourget airport in Paris.

He and his single engine Spirit of St. Louis, was welcomed and cheered by two hundred thousand people.

That was only the start of it, as his return to New York gathered some four million to welcome him as a hero.

We all know what tragedies he later suffered, but he will forever be remembered for his brave achievement.

Flying high above Germany I can't help thinking about today being the memorial day of the Holocaust, the fifty-sixth.

Only a few survivors are still alive to talk about it.

What I can't understand is that even today you find a lot of people who either defend what happened, or denies that it ever happened.

Six million people were deliberately killed for either being Jews, Gypsies or homosexuals, so-called "Untermenschen" in the eyes of the Nazies.

Auschwitz, Treblinka, Buchenwald, Dachau, Bergen Belsen, and would you believe it, close to a hundred camps only in Germany if I am not wrong, and many more in all of the German occupied countries.

When I was in my twenties, I visited Bergen Belsen together with a couple of people from the Norwegian resistance during the war, and that was an unforgettable experience.

Snowfilled Norway

Change of temperature is one thing, but from a green winter in Southern Spain, with still around fifteen degrees Celsius above or more in the shade, and only rarely down to 10 at night, to a snowy winter in Norway, is close to a shock.

However, I am used to these changes as I frequently travel between Norway and Southern Spain. It is important to stress that I am talking about Southern Spain, as that is the only place on mainland Europe where the sun spends the winter.

This statement is not quite true, as there are only certain places in Andalucia with a micro climate which justify using that expression.

Last year was the worst year I can remember weatherwise. It seemed like the whole world had been turned upside down. Generally it was much warmer in the north and colder in the south than before, and with lots of floods and winds.

Even my sister in Australia was complaining about the unusual weather.

In Norway people say that there is no such thing as bad weather, it is only a matter of how you dress. This is fair enough I think, and a much more positive attitude than to complain about it.

To see my two grandsons enjoying the snow is great. The older one, at four and a half, is already on his own on the slopes, and I understand that he now also manages the ski lift by himself.

His kindergarten is situated on the top of the hill north of Oslo, about four hundred meters above sea level.

If you have heard about the famous ski-jump, Holmenkollen, it is only a little higher up.

Every day, weather allowing, they are out in the woods playing and, of course, skiing.

To get there every morning, either my daughter or my son-in-law will drive him to the nearby tram station, from where he will, together with a bunch of other children, take the tram up to the top.

When I was here in October last year, it happened a few times that we, on the way to the office, drove him all the way up.

Once, on a very foggy day, while my son-in-law took him from the car-park to one of the huts belonging to the kindergarten, an elk, a Norwegian moose, crossed the road in front of the car and stopped just less than ten meters from it and started nibbling on the leaves of a birch tree.

For close to ten minutes he was standing there, and only when my son-in-law returned, did he slowly move into the woods.

It was not a very big one, but still he measured about two meters to the top of his small antlers, obviously a calf.

If it had been a nice Sunday I am sure we would have all been up there skiing, but overcast and foggy as it is I think we will rather take a walk just to get some fresh air.

The younger one at two and a half, goes to a kindergarten just a few hundred meters from where they live. He has not yet started skiing, but it seems like I will have the pleasure of seeing him try for the first time next Saturday or Sunday.

Tanks Escape   *Jan Arnt 2017*

Rotary Club

My Rotary Club in Oslo where I have been a member since it was chartered on the eight of May 1986, has its meetings on Mondays.

As most of the members don't live in this area, but have their work around here, the meetings take place at lunchtime. You may or may not know, but being a Rotarian you are supposed to be present at minimum sixty percent of the meetings, but not necessarily at your own club.

Due to the fact that I live in Spain I have far from been able to live up to this percentage in the last years, and unfortunately there are no clubs in the area where I live making it impossible for me to compensate.

I make it a point to always go to the meetings when I am in Norway.

There is one other member of the club in the same situation as me, but we have both up to now been given the possibility to remain members even if we don't live up to the sixty percent attendance rule.

For many years now women have been admitted as members of the Rotary, providing the club members have voted in favour of it.

This already happened years ago in our club, but only a few have since become members.

Anyhow, our club, Furuset Rotary Club in Oslo, has never exceeded thirty members and today, we have only one woman member.

From my start as a Rotarian I have always been against women members.

They have their own clubs, as for instance the Inner Wheel, so why can't men have their Rotary clubs for themselves.

I am not against women in Rotary because I do not like women, nor do I in any way discriminate against them.

In my business I have always encouraged women to go for important positions, both as sales and finance managers.

The reason for my reluctance to see women as members of the Rotary is that I openly admit that when women are present in a room I automatically behave in a slightly different manner than I would only amongst men.

This should only be seen as a compliment to women.

During the meeting today, a female manager of a public institution made a speech about young trainees in practical jobs and how society organizes this.

To make a long story short, one of her conclusions was that many of these youngsters have great difficulties adapting to a practical responsible life, because of their general lack of basic manners.

What most of us take for granted as manners, and think we have passed on to our children while educating them, is something which does not exist everywhere.

What your parents do not teach you about manners while you are growing up, you will simply start life without and it is not likely that you will obtain it later. On the contrary, you will be an easy victim for influences of all kinds.

Last week a sixteen year old coloured boy was stabbed and killed in Oslo by some youngsters from the New Nazi movement just because he was of another race. Discrimination happens all the time, but this was one of the many incidents which ended in a tragic way. Police and witnesses said it was cold-blooded murder.

The extremist group behind it call themselves the Boot Boys, and they are well known to the police for their threatening behaviour towards people of all kinds from the third world.

Keep Norway clean, they say.

Our democracy and freedom of speech I can both understand and appreciate, but the lack of laws for the police to stop this kind of extremist activity I cannot understand and never will.

Any politician delving into this matter and demanding stronger reactions is in deep trouble in this country and will be branded racist.

My opinion is that tolerance in this matter has gone far too far and that something radical must be done while there is still a chance.

All this because my flight over Germany the other day is still fresh in my mind.

Despite slimming and having changed my diet, my doctor put me on pills to lower the blood pressure.

Golf Academy

I have been wondering if my high blood pressure may be caused by the frustration I have with my golf. I have heard that in the United States a lot of people go to their shrinks with similar frustrations. Once I thought I had a certain grip on my golf, but after having spent two days at the Leadbetter Golf Academy, about one and a half years ago, I never seem to have got back what I once had.

I have been down to 8.1 in handicap, but that was back in ninety-seven.

Well, I have no shrink as I have never been to one, and I don't think this is the time to look for one.

The first thing we humans do when something goes wrong is to blame it on someone or something else, saying to ourselves that the fault is not ours.

In my earlier days when shooting clay pigeons, I also did quite a bit of coaching.

Often when newcomers to the game asked advice about what kind of shotgun they should buy, I told them that as a beginner, the choice is of little importance. What matters is the man who pull the trigger, I said.

If, at a later stage you should find out that you really want to go for the sport, then that's the time to go into details about the equipment.

To substantiate this point I quite often, while teaching, used my very first Spanish built AYA side by side shotgun which I got when I was fourteen, and not my Italian Perazzi which is specially designed for skeet shooting.

That was quite a few years ago, but here I find myself in a similar silly situation. In my frustration I consider buying a new set of golf clubs, although I am presently using a set of Callaways which I bought only five years ago.

At this time of the year there is no way that you can play golf in Norway apart from in a place called Hemsedal, where they have a winter course for playing on snow with red balls.

Flying an hour down to the south of Sweden or to Denmark you can still play on most of the courses, but no one is that crazy.

If Norwegians want to play golf in the winter, they go much farther south.

Indoor golf centres with driving ranges are very popular here, so I decided to borrow my friend's new set of Taylor Made clubs, to try them, and to see if they were better than mine. He could eventually get me a similar set at a wholesale price.

At lunchtime I drove down to his office to collect the clubs.

I think I will never understand big business, and to be frank I have limited interest in really trying. Nokia, the Finnish company, or is it really Finnish, produced 128 million mobile phones last year and made a profit of around eight billion dollars.

As this information was made public, their shares went down 8 percent.

They see a bright future ahead, and claim they have investigated in possible alternative production facilities around the world.

However, they have come to the conclusion that they are the best, and therefore will keep the production in Finland.

Ericsson, the Swedish Communication Company produced 43 million mobiles last year and declared that they will stop all their own production, because they have a substantial loss on each mobile they produce.

The world market for mobiles next year was estimated not too long ago, to be more than half a billion units sold, but now the estimates have been somewhat reduced I understand.

Is it frightening or not, that only eight percent of news information in Norway is related to out of the country matters? I wonder what similar statistics show in the various countries within the European Community. I think it is more than frightening if they are on the same level as in Norway.

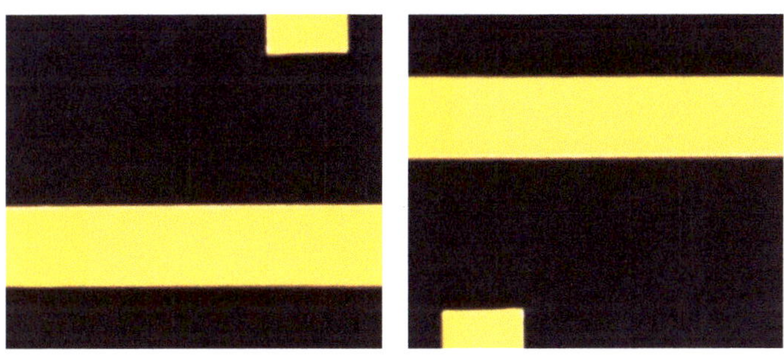

False thoughts   *Jan Arnt 2017*

Daily planning

The morning ritual at my daughter and son-in-law's is somewhat unusual for the grandpa of the two kids. We are all up at seven o'clock, but that is only officially. As I live in my own quarters just two doors away from the boys' room, I quite often hear them making noise in the middle of the night.

I have a suspicion that every now and then there is some up and down traffic during the night.

When I have finished preparing myself for the day, and skimmed through the two papers they get delivered in the morning, I will go up the stairs to find the family sitting at the kitchen table having their breakfast.

As far as I can understand, there are no fixed rules about who drives the kids to their kindergartens. That is something they decide according to whatever obligations they have at the office, as they both work under the same roof.

Maybe it is very different with boys than with girls, or maybe it is my memory.

Anyhow, I cannot remember anything close to the same kind of behaviour when my two girls grew up.

The boys are lovely, but they sure know how to get their point across about what they like or dislike, mostly the latter.

Then again, I must say, when it is twenty below and you have to get their clothes ready, just dressing them is a physical challenge.

The last thing is to put cream in their faces to protect them against the cold, before we are all ready to walk down the four flights of stairs with their rucksacks, the rubbish bags, and whatever we happen to be carrying to and from the office.

Lately they have luckily been able to rent a private parking place just across the street, for one of their cars, whereas the other one is to be found wherever a parking space was to be had the day before, normally not more than a few hundred meters away.

On this particular morning they, for one reason or another, split up.

I was to drive with my daughter and the younger one, while my son-in-law took the older one.

Although there is almost no snow in the town itself at this time, it is still quite icy, making me walk as if I were way past seventy.

Going around the corner, my daughter, carrying the little one, stumbled just as she was approaching the car. As she was falling forward with the child close to her chest, I just managed to put myself in a position where she could fall against my outstretched arm. Apart from the kid screaming, I think more from shock than pain, no one was hurt except my poor back which was twisted.

Luckily for me, precisely because of my bad back, I had booked a massage for later in the afternoon.

I do understand that my daughter and son-in-law at times are fed up with the constant noise from the children, but I think they are still far from joining the parents in the American survey which shows that people over there are generally more pleased with their cars than with their children.

They say that the trial about the Lockerbie bombing on December twenty-first nineteen-eighty- eight, killing two hundred and seventy people, lasted nine months and cost one hundred million dollars. That was the infamous Pan Am flight 103.

Abdelbaset al-Megrahi, forty-eight, was found guilty by three Scottish judges, and given life in prison, while Al-Amin Khalifa Fhimah forty-four, was acquitted.

Thirteen years it took to get this far so let us hope it was a fair trial and not as some are speculating, an arranged compromise.

After my massage, I went with my daughter to one of the indoor driving ranges in Oslo. We shared one hundred and forty balls, and when I asked her to look at my swing, and particularly what to look for, I quickly realized that I would not benefit from buying a new set of golf clubs after all.

Surviver

Eleven years ago today the funeral of my eldest daughter Nicoline took place. Needless to say, just thinking about it, brings back a lot of feelings. As my son-in-law is in Sweden today on business, I am alone at home with the children and my daughter. The little ones are in bed, and the two of us are celebrating a significant verbal order we got today in our neighbouring country.

When we get it confirmed in writing, it will probably be the largest single order we have ever got in the history of our company.

Logically we talked about Nicoline and as we had a few glasses of white wine, memories were brought up.

She died on January the twenty-sixth nineteen-ninety, 27 years old, while my younger daughter was studying economics in Madrid.

She is telling me that on January the twenty-fifth she was in her car on the way back from Navacerrada, a ski resort one hour out of Madrid.

She was with her boyfriend, Jose Maria, and another friend, Roderic, from Holland. On the radio they heard Michael Bolton playing and singing "I am a survivor".

They all sang it for Nicoline again and again, all the way back to Madrid.

She remembers, as if it were yesterday, calling us the minute she got home.

She got me on the phone she recalls, only to be told to get on a plane back to Norway the next day. She also remember asking me to call if something happened, and me answering something like: "I don't know".

I do not remember any of this, but for her it is crystal clear.

Early the next day she went to the Barajas Airport to buy a ticket, only to find that there was no coverage on her credit card or that the line to the bank was down.

When she asked the clerk to call the bank, she was answered: "I'm not obliged to do so". She then told him about her situation and why it was so urgent to get to Norway, after which there was no problem, "ningun problema".

Full speed ahead, first to Barcelona and then to what should have been Copenhagen.

Due to a storm, the plane to Copenhagen could not take off, and was three hours delayed.

She tells me that she had started crying and that a man came up to her and asked if there was anything he could do. She told him about her sister, after which the man introduced himself as a doctor going to Oslo for a seminar. He invited her for lunch and calmed her down. She then called my office to tell me about the delay.

As I was not in the office, for obvious reasons, she told the girl at the switchboard to tell me about the delay.

The doctor was then the best person to get back to in her present situation, she remembers.

Arriving at the airport in Oslo where I met her, she told me about the doctor, and only then that her mother had told her about Nicoline's death the night before.

Her mother has been living, and still is, in the south of Spain, about four hours from where I live, since we divorced about twenty years ago.

She called my daughter this morning, from a hospital in Malaga, to tell her that she had got some trouble with her leg.

With all due respect for the coloured boy who was killed the other day, it seems like the whole nation now have got their eyes opened to the danger of the New Nazi movement.

More than forty thousand people were on the streets of Oslo demonstrating against racism, and paying tribute to the young boy. That means that almost one tenth of all the inhabitants of the capital took part.

This is the largest gathering of people in Oslo since liberation day at the end of the second world war fifty-six years ago, apart from a few times during Holmenkollen skiing events.

The same happened in many, many other cities all over Norway.

Cigar

In the Philippines they are struggling with a lot of things, but apparently obesity is also a big problem. Singing and eating are their number one and two favourites. Singing I can imagine only makes them happy, but as a consequence of the eating they have become world leaders in using medicine to reduce weight.

Personally I believe that taking medicine is only one way to lose weight, the best is, and will always be to eat less.

However, like with smoking, the problem is not to stop, the problem is to not start again.

Someone said that women are like cigars; their fire has to be lit often.

I think that is very true, but what about us men?

Doesn't our fire also need to be lit every now and then?

I believe women who understand this, lead happier lives than those who don't.

A good balance I suppose will give the best result.

As I had two daughters I should maybe have thought about it, but do you not, like me, think that statistically there must be just as many girls born as boys in this world. Correct or not, that the balance is kept is in it self fantastic, but then nature is wonderful.

According to reports presented today, Norwegian fighter pilots are questioning the birth statistics somewhat.

The report says that from nineteen ninety-seven, till today, these high-flying fast guys are producing sixty-two and a half percent daughters.

The fact is that there are more boys born than girls in the world.

I suppose that nature over time has seen that men are the ones who fight wars, and die, and also that men in general live shorter then women.

Something like that must be the reason why more boys than girls are being born.

Then, what is causing these fighter pilots to produce more girls than boys?

Questions are now being asked if it has something to do with the G-force they are exposed to, or maybe electromagnetic forces.

Well, a serious investigation is under way I understand.

I never was a fighter pilot, but still managed to make a hundred percent female contribution instead of sixty-two and a half percent.

Humans can't easily change nature.

The United States are reducing the interest rate for the second time this year, to a total of one percent, and here the banks are lending out money like never before. An increase of fourteen percent compared with last year they say, simultaneously admitting that their solidity would be much better if the increase did not exceed ten percent.

I called a friend of mine at his cabin in the mountains. They were having a lovely time with beautiful sunny weather and twenty-seven degrees Celsius below, freezing.

Peace thoughts

Electricity

Power is important in almost all situations, and one can really get frightened thinking about what happened to the electricity situation in California. A few years ago, I remember that our Danish lawyer was travelling a lot to the west coast of the United States. It all had to do with windmills and he, as I understood it, together with some other lawyers represented the Danish company which had produced and delivered a vast amount of them over there.

They were placed outside Los Angeles, and a court case was held against the Danish manufacturer because the windmills did not deliver power according to their specifications.

It was, as I understood it, only minimal discrepancies but enough for the customer to refuse paying for them.

I think the case went on for years, and no doubt, the cost involved by the lawyers on either side was enormous.

Who in the end won the case I don't know, but surely the big winners must have been, as always, the lawyers.

It is very difficult to understand that in a country like the United States of America, a situation like this, where they simply are not able to deliver enough electricity, can occur.

I am all for privatization, but are looking forward to hearing if it will ever be known to the public, how they managed to get into such a miserable situation related to their electricity supply.

In one of these programs on television where they are testing products and comparing their quality, they made a comparison between different types of torch batteries.

I am probably not the only one having had bad experiences with batteries.

At home we have power-cuts every now and then. The slightest bit of rain and one can rest assured that there will be a cut. The cuts normally do not last very long, but when you get them, you had better be prepared.

Torches are only one of many battery consuming implements in our home.

I will tell you about another one which in my opinion is very rare. I have never elsewhere seen a gadget like the one we are using in conjunction with our door bell.

That may not be so strange, as I have thought it up and installed it myself. We have a kind of a tower to bring us from the parking level to the terrace. Five stories high it is, prepared with a lift shaft, and stairs.

We have for a long time been saying that we should install a lift, but climbing the fifty-six steps is very good training and helps us keep fit, and it has also been a matter of economic priorities. Instead of a lift we have an electrical winch with a basket, in the shaft, to bring up whatever we need. So far we have not had a power-cut happen while operating the winch, but what if we had a lift installed? What would then happen if the power went off with us both in it? The supplier, who has given us an estimate for a lift, guarantees that if such a situation should occur, it will slowly glide down to the ground floor, and the doors will open automatically.

Well, back to the gadget for the door bell. I have installed a chain in the lift shaft, which, sliding over a couple of wheels, runs from the outside wall beside the front door on the parking level, up to a brass bell on the top floor about fifteen meters above. A spring smooths the action when you pull it, and it works perfectly. The only problem is that when we are inside the house, the sound of the brass bell cannot be heard, even if the sound in itself is pretty high.

To overcome this problem I found a little battery-operated transmitter and receiver. The transmitter I mounted into a little box with a metal arm sticking out as a switch. This is then connected to the chain, and voilà, when pulling the chain the transmitter is activated.

After carefully trying out how far away the receiver with a buzzer could be mounted, I found a place almost in direct line behind the curtains in the dining room. The snag is now only that the transmitter and receiver must be kept on constantly to work, and that requires frequent changes of batteries.

The above mentioned battery test caught my immediate interest as you can imagine. Of all of them, the Panasonic energizer came out a definite leader.

They cost four ninety-five Norwegian kroner a piece, and lasted seven hours during the specific test they made.

They would save eight hundred kroner yearly for a Walkman user, they said. I will be happy if I, after changing to this type of battery on my special door bell, will be able to change them every second month, instead of every month as I do now.

An hour:

An hour seems never to end-
when you are just around the bend.
GM

Flourishing thoughts   *Jan Arnt 2017*

Evening paper

A Swedish evening paper writes that Norway is a half crazy Viking country. I did not catch what they meant by the expression, but in many ways I feel it is correct. Things here tend to be dealt with in a far from traditional way. When things have gone too far, the Norwegians very often deal with the matter by making a so called "skippertak".

The expression covers what happens when everyone gets together to make an all-out effort to solve a specific problem there and then. The idea in itself is not bad, but as I said, a "skippertak" is only made when things have already gone too far, which means that it should not have been necessary at all if the planning and preparation had been better in the first place. The other thing is that when a "skippertak" has been made, everyone feels satisfied and goes back to the original routines.

There is, of course, much more to it than this simple example, but the "skippertak", I think, really characterizes the Norwegian way of solving problems.

In business we find the Swedes much better organized than ourselves.

I am not so sure that the average Norwegian will agree with me, but this is an observation I have made over many years.

They have a long tradition as industrialists and in international business in general.

We started up with a new agent in Sweden from the first of January this year. He is supposed to market our digital dictation systems and we feel confident that it will be successful.

We have already prepared the Swedish market for some time, and particularly the largest hospital in the capital Stockholm.

They have had a digital dictation system on trial for almost a year and seem to be quite satisfied both with the functionality and the follow up from our side. They are indeed so satisfied, that we this morning got verbal information saying that they will go for our system in the whole hospital.

This, when we get it in writing, will probably be the largest order our company have ever got from one single customer.

"Life is not what has happened, but what you remember, and the way you remember it".

Gabriel Garcia Marquez who wrote these words is now writing his autobiography "Living to Tell the Tale".

Born on March the sixth, nineteen twenty-eight, he was one of sixteen children, just imagine, and ended up getting the Nobel price in literature in eighty-two.

I think his words are so very true. I find it easy to accept that in most cases there will be a discrepancy between what happened and what you remember, but I think his adding of a new dimension "the way you remember it" says a lot about his character.

He should certainly know something about it, as I understand that he in most of his writing refers to stories he has been told.

My daughter and son-in-law have been looking for a house for quite some time.

Living in a flat in town with two small boys is no problem in itself now before they start going to school, but in a couple of years when the older one does, a lot of things will change.

I must admit I feel ill when I see the level of house prices in Oslo but then of course, I compare them with what they were like when I was in that market many years ago, what I remember from that time, and logically, the way I remember it.

I believe there is a kind of proportion in everything, for instance between the cost and your income, and the mortgage you can live with in proportion to the same.

They are looking for a fairly big house, a place where they can stay until they, maybe when they are getting old, want to move back to a flat.

Well, she, at least, has made up her mind more or less about where she wants to live.

He would, I believe, not mind being a little more flexible about that, but she is so far managing to stay firm about it, without it seeming to create any serious confrontations between them.

Cuevas de Almanzora, a small town about half an hour's drive from us in Spain, used to be a mining town. At the turn of the century more people were living there than in the city of Almeria, the capital of this part of Andalucia.

They say that tens of thousands of people were living in cave houses in those days, and quite a few still are. I have been there to have a closer look at these kinds of cave houses, and can well understand they must have been both practical, and in many ways ideal.

Inside temperatures varied very little from winter to summer, and when they expected more children, they just dug out a new room.

Not so any more, even in Oslo you must be prepared to heat a house to cope with up to thirty degrees Celsius below zero and if you want to add a room or more you must first get your planning through the bureaucracy, then the building permission and finally you must be prepared to spend a bomb having it built.

By the way, to day it's about twenty below

Spanish thoughts

Snowboard course

This is the day when my daughter was to start a snowboard course. She bought her set of board, boots and protection equipment on Saturday, and was both prepared and eager to start today. Two of her close girlfriends were also to start, and they were all looking forward to spending this time away from their kids.

I can certainly see how "cool" she will become in the eyes of the boys, her sons, when she joins them on the slopes one day.

When calling to check on the meeting point, she was told that they had to cancel because it was already twenty degrees Celsius below zero, and that it later in the evening most probably would fall to around twenty-five.

Because of the short days most ski slopes in this country are lit up enabling people to use them at off-work hours, both in the mornings and in the evenings.

Twenty to twenty-five below is cold, but you can imagine what that feels like when the wind is blowing. At only fifteen below zero, but with a wind of an average strong force, the effect of the cold against the skin is equal to thirty-two below.

Not strange that they tell parents to protect their children with cream, or not to let them out during periods with these kinds of temperatures.

Even grown-ups have to be careful.

The coldest place in Norway last night was a place called Drevsjø at forty-three and a half below. Imagine that situation combined with wind. Today the annual dogsled race is taking place in that area, the so called "Femundsløpet".

About one thousand megawatts are imported by Denmark to cope with the consumption of electricity in the country. It has been colder in earlier years, but the consumption has never been so high as it is nowadays.

Today it will most probably pass twenty-three thousand two-hundred megawatts, while the absolute maximum available, reserves included, is twenty-four thousand.

The politicians are happy, as more than fifty percent of the bill charged to the consumer is going into their pockets in the form of taxes.

I wonder what the temperature is today in Tatarstan, one of the Russian republics. Not that I have any personal interests in it, but we have seen what a lot of people have to cope with over there, with power- cuts up to twelve hours a day.

Even if it is cold and they have power-cuts, Marija Vasilijeva, age one hundred and four, is growing new teeth I read, very much to the astonishment of the doctors. As she lives on vegetables and chicken, she can now chew her food.

During one of her many visits to our family cabin, my eldest daughter with some friends once had a special experience.

This happened one January in the middle of the eighties. They had an average of thirty-six degrees below zero throughout the whole week they were there. The cabin is situated on a peninsula in a lake, one thousand meters above sea level.

The cabin is equipped with both running water and electricity, and is quite functional.

I don't really understand how they could enjoy skiing at those temperatures, but they were all sporty and every day they went to the downhill slopes on the other side of the lake.

One day they came back to the cabin and found that the power had gone.

Imagine, from the time they left the nice, warm cabin in the morning, until they returned in the afternoon, the water boiler inside the cabin had frozen, pipes had broken and water had poured all over the floors. Now they found that all the floors were covered in ice.

Luckily enough the electricity came back on a short while later.

The ice melted slowly as they got the cabin warmed up, and for them it was an unforgettable experience.

After hearing stories like this one, I understand that our power-cuts in Spain are something we can learn to live with, as the worst that can happen over time is that the food in the freezer gets ruined.

Fortunately, it has not happened so far that we have had to throw away any ruined food for this reason.

Two thoughts

UNICEF

It is a common understanding among Norwegians that children in this country are very well protected compared with children in other countries. This, however, is not at all the fact as I understand it. According to statistics released today by UNICEF, Norway is in fifth place. Sweden is the leader in this respect and obviously then the country where children are safest.

We are talking about children up to twelve years old, killed in all kinds of accidents such as traffic, fire, drowning, etc.

One dead child is, of course, one too many, but there will always be accidents, whatever is done to prevent them from happening.

Norwegian politicians were surprised when confronted with these figures, as they also thought we would be much better off, but they will get in touch with the Swedes they say, to find out what they are doing and what not.

Cars and traffic is often up for discussion, and here there are as many opinions as there are people. I think that even if they don't admit it, most people look at themselves as having the best idea about how the traffic-rules should be.

Norway has from the first of January this year changed its law about alcohol and driving. The level was lowered from 0.5 to 0.2. This means that if you are not a nervous wreck already, you are likely to become one now.

That is, of course, only related to those of us who do not mind having a glass of wine to go with our meals.

0.2 means the same as zero. The problem is then, always having to count how many hours before driving you can have your last glass of wine.

In no way do I approve of drinking and driving, and I think it is important to have clear rules about it. No one is talking about how you drive, as your driving skills are never taken into consideration. I suppose that would be impossible anyway, as the rules and regulations must be the same for everyone.

The speed limit here has been ninety on certain motorways, though it is normally eighty, eighty on the good roads and so on, downwards.

Now they will increase the speed on the real motorways to a hundred, while on most of the eighty roads it will be reduced to seventy.

It costs a fortune to make these changes as you can imagine, since tens of thousands of signs will have to be changed.

I am not so sure I feel confident that changes like these will lead to fewer accidents, as most of us will continue to drive according to the circumstances anyhow.

I hope only few people react like me in the traffic. Just seeing a policeman makes me nervous, as I have a feeling that they are after me. In that respect I feel better off driving in Spain.

No reason why I should have such a reaction, as I have never had any problems with the police, but I still have this feeling.

Well, one of my sayings is that there is no future without a past. Let's hope that they have learnt something from their previous experience with the alcohol law, as well as with the speed limits, and that the changes they have now made will be for the good of all of us.

In Israel, Ariel Sharon, the hawk and veteran terrorist is now leading with sixty-two percent to Ehud Barak's, thirty-seven. Apparently many people are boycotting the election they say, in protest against both candidates. The final result will most likely come tomorrow, but there is no doubt about who will win.

How long Sharon will be the prime minister remains to be seen, however.

The ethnic minority in Norway, "Samene", (the Laplanders), are celebrating their National Day today.

The official Norwegian National Day is May the seventeenth.

Time:

**It`s not important what time it is-
what`s important is that it passes.
GM**

Mr. No

My daughter was more successful today. The weather has changed totally, it started snowing, and the snowboard course was on. She looked very happy and enthusiastic when she took off. As she was dressed for skiing and left with the new board, it became too much for the little one. It was not to be expected that he would understand that he was not joining her, even if it was at six o'clock in the afternoon.

He started screaming like I do not know what, and there was no way he could be comforted for at least half an hour. The older one had heard and understood that she was going on this course, and had no problem with her leaving.

On the contrary, he saw that it was important for her to learn it, so they could later go together.

How is it that "no" is the first word little kids learn? To me it's quite logical, as it is the first word parents hammer into their little heads.

Strange though, when kids have built up a real anger, they will say no to any suggestion you come up with, while trying to stop them screaming. At times they will even say no when you in between threats of various kinds, suggest a biscuit or a piece of chocolate.

There are many people who grow up and stay like that.

Was it Molotov they called Mr. No?

A lot of scientists are working with the development of robots, and every now and then you can read about artificial intelligence which could outmanoeuvre humans.

In other words, we could be controlled by them, and not as we would like to see it in future, us controlling them.

We would like to see them as ideal helpers doing all the dirty work that we would rather like others to do.

Professor Kevin Warwick is one of the scientists doing research on the subject.

He has just finalized an experiment where he implanted a little chip in his arm. It was to transmit information from his nerves.

After six weeks it was taken out again, and apparently the experiment must have been successful, as he now is going to implant a larger and more sophisticated chip.

Information transmitted by radio from people with these kinds of implants could apparently help many disabled people.

If his latest experiment turns out to be successful, his intention is to do a similar implant on his wife.

They should then, according to his visions, be able to exchange feelings via radio, and he is quite prepared for the possibility that they will be able to feel each other's pain.

He mentioned that even one's sex-life could be improved, without mentioning if it could get worse if it was already good.

Personally I am in no doubt that it one day will become quite natural to implant chips in our bodies, to be used for practical improvements of our daily life. However, I am just as worried about the possible negative sides of such development, and the way it might be misused.

Anyhow, his conclusion is that these experiments were not without danger, but he felt that it was something he had to carry on with.

His aim is to one day make people able to communicate by thoughts.

I can only see this as an option, as I believe that verbal and physical communication will always make the best forms for contact.

Security guards at the White House in Washington have been put on high alert as there has been some shooting outside the building. A young man was discovered with a handgun, was shot in the leg and taken into custody.

Neither the president nor his family, or anyone else in the building, was hurt.

Many thoughts Jan Arnt 2017

Crossing thoughts Jan Arnt 2017

Lucky Number

The peace process in the Middle East, the continuation of the so-called Oslo Agreement, seems to be in great danger. I doubt that anyone believe that the negotiations will continue, or be carried on with any great hopes of their being successful. Ariel Sharon has already been at the wall in Jerusalem, and while he was there he claimed that it should belong to the Israelis for ever more. This is a clear and very diplomatic statement, surely a good basis for successful peace negotiations with the Palestinians.

If I was not who I am, I could have been successful at playing the stock exchange. I know a lot of people whose daily behaviour depends entirely on the various daily indexes.

When the Dow Jones is up they meet the day with a smile, you can almost see their brains silently calculating their profits.

When it is down they also look down as they in despair calculate their losses, while you have to cheer them up, trying to convince them that after all the money is not lost before they sell. Unfortunately it is the same with the profit; it is not there before you have sold your shares.

I understand, of course, that the stock exchange is important, it is the hub in the spinning wheel of economics, but it is only that for me it has never been an option for how to manage my economy.

That may very well be the reason why I am not a rich man after more than 40 active years in business. I have had plenty of challenges and worries in my life, but fortunately not from playing the stock exchange. I have never got my kicks from gambling, although I have tried it a few times.

Once, during a visit to the factories whose products we represented in Norway, just a few years after my school-time in Italy at the same factory, I had a fantastic experience.

I was there for a few days trying to create interest in a new development we had made in the field of typewriters. I was introduced to the head of the patent department, a pleasant elderly person, and as he knew I was alone, he introduced me to his beautiful secretary, more or less my age.

I had rented a little Fiat six hundred for the days I was there, and was prepared to invite her for dinner.

As I was, from my earlier school-times in the same area, quite knowledgeable about the good places, I invited her to a lovely restaurant in a village almost an hour's drive up the Aosta Valley.

On the way we passed the Casino in Saint-Vincent, where I had only been once before, just watching, not playing.

To make an impression on this lovely little Italian secretary, I invited her to join me for a closer look inside.

Passport and identification had to be presented before we could enter into this holy playground. Wandering around and having a look at the various possibilities, one of the big roulette tables caught my eye.

As if I had done little more then play my whole life, I went up to the table, made an excuse to squeeze in between a couple of fat cigar-smoking Milanese, and put my entire stake on number fourteen.

Would you believe it, fourteen came up as the winner and I got thirty-six times my stake. The little secretary almost fainted while I, shocked as well but still trying to keep a straight face, collected my winnings and told her it was time to leave, after all we were going for dinner.

After a lovely meal in a restaurant called The Three Kings, translated into English, in a nearby little town, where only the best on the menu was selected, we drove home.

As she was living with her parents and I was staying in a hotel where mainly people related to the factory were staying, we spent quite some time in the little Fiat six-hundred, overlooking the lights of the town and the river passing through it.

I never met her again, but I feel sure that she had also had an unforgettable evening.

I don't think that the thirtieth anniversary of the NASDAQ today was a very happy one, but then again, a yo-yo is supposed to go up and down, isn't it.

Wild animals

Chasing wolves is something that can really turn people on. Already before I left home for Norway, it was all over the papers in Spain. The barbaric Norwegians were going to kill the few wolves in the country, instead of letting them live to kill sheep. Things might have been different if the wolves killed only to eat, but it seems that they also just kill for fun, and at times I understand they slaughter ten or fifteen sheep there and then and just leave them.

Yes, also the bears, which there are a few of in certain areas of the country, will feed from these woollen delicacies. I think most of us believe that bears are vegetarians, mostly feeding on berries, but a bear can also be a killer, doing it for fun.

So you see it is not only people who appreciate a good leg of lamb.

The farmers are the ones complaining and the ones who suffer. Before they could blame the wolves it was the bears.

God knows how much the state have paid to the farmers over the last decades as compensation for lost sheep, and for outsiders like me, with limited knowledge of these things, it seems as if the woods must be filled with wolves and bears to do so much damage.

According to what we can read in the papers, however, there are only a few in the whole country.

Of course, wolves, like all animals who feed on meat, cannot all of a sudden turn into vegetarians.

As they are pretty smart they go for an easy kill. Few animals are easier to catch than the stupid sheep, I am afraid. In Norway they are, in the summertime, let out to graze and will stay outside the entire season, provided of course that they are not killed by wolves or bears.

By the way, flying home from Norway last time, I brought with me a smoked leg of lamb. I admit that a Spanish "Pata Negra" ham is the best thing you can serve me, but the Norwegian smoked leg of lamb, together with a small aquavit, "Linjeakevitt", and so-called flat bread, "Flatbrød", do tempt me to change my mind. Well, the debate about shooting or not shooting the wolves have been going on for quite a while, and several alternative suggestions have been brought forward.

"Nordmarka", the woods north of Oslo, actually starting on the doorstep of my elder grandson's kindergarten, have been suggested as a place to put the wolves. What is the argument in favour of that you may ask?

It is probably because in these woods there are no sheep, only thousands of people from Oslo using them for hiking both summer and winter.

These woods contain a lot of elks, the Norwegian moose, and they are normally too big for the wolves to catch. Logical isn't it?

I don't need to mention that the female minister seriously suggesting it belongs to a different political ideology than I do.

To catch the wolves and transfer them would be a difficult task anyhow, so in the meantime they have decided to kill I think six of them.

The hunt started today with a lot of international and national press following every step of the hunt.

The area they are searching to find them covers about seven hundred square kilometres, so let us see what happens.

There have also been a lot of discussions about using helicopters, but so far I think that the protesters have won that argument of fair play. Well, if they want to move them, the only way to put them to sleep is to do it from the air.

The good thing for the hunters is that they will all get one month's pay from the state, whether or not they find and kill the wolves.

The color is red

Icon

An icon is something I am sure most youngsters working with computers know about. I believe anyone working with computers, knows that the small pictures on the screen which are used to activate the various programmes are called icons, not only the youngsters.

The difference between the youngsters and the more mature among us may be that the more mature will know that an icon is also a picture with religious motive, and normally of Russian origin as far as I know. The fact is that an icon could be just any kind of picture; it's only that we normally don't use the expression, icon, about ordinary pictures.

The reason icons normally portray holy men and women, is to constantly remind their owners about the actual Saint portrayed, and I suppose that they are more in use where religion forms an active part of everyday life, than otherwise.

Next time, if you have not observed it, and you take a taxi in a Latin country, look for the picture of a Saint in the car. You will be surprised how often you will find the driver's icon.

I am of the opinion that pictures should be visible. This is logical when we are talking about paintings, they are visible, and for me they only have meaning when they are displayed.

If I think about the amount of photographs I have stored away and very seldom look at, I feel in a way sorry. I know they are there, but in a way keeping them there is the same as saying: "Out of sight out of mind".

Anyhow, in my office, or rather our office at home, the walls are packed with framed photographs, constantly reminding us about highlights of various kinds. Pictures of the time we planted a tree or a bush, and then pictures of the same tree or bush a few years later. You don't need the two to remind yourself about the evolution, of course, but it sure gives you a good feeling to look at them.

As well, it gives a special feeling to look at our house when it was surrounded by pine trees, and then at the picture taken after the great fire in August nineteen ninety-nine, when they were all gone.

New trees planted, new challenges and new pictures.

There are times when I, for reasons unknown, will see a picture in my mind's eye and drift off. Memories are brought back, and I suppose it is for this reason we love to take pictures.

We need something to look at later, to bring back memories.

Around ten degrees below today, but with a completely clear blue sky, and no wind.

This was the time to go skiing with the kids. We went to the slopes just beside my older grandson's kindergarten.

I have never seen so many cars parked in that area, or so many people.

On the way driving up there, we passed trams filled with people. Each of them was packed, and not even one more person could have got into them.

As it was my first time to see my older grandson on skis, I had of course brought my camera.

The younger one, at two and a half, has not yet got his skis, but I think he will later this season.

When you experience a day like this and see how people enjoy the outdoors, I must admit that the quality of life in this country must be among the best in the whole world, providing you like a country with four very distinct seasons.

I know that as soon as I have developed the film in my camera, one or two of the pictures will be enlarged and framed, and will hang among all the others in the office at home, giving me the greatest pleasure to look at for years to come.

Pocket Memo

To me it's quite strange. Earlier I found it very easy to make my reflections by dictating them straight into my Pocket Memo and transcribing them at a later stage. Since I started writing these "Thoughts", I have found it easier to write them down directly without dictating them first. This is a strange situation for me to be in, as I never thought I could do it this way.

On the other hand, the few writers I have met, all type everything directly without using dictation.

I once made, with good help from a colleague, a complete concept of a procedure for taking notes, organizing them, dictating the content and typing it out. I called it the "Brain Manager", and was actually quite proud of it.

I used it for a year or two, among other things for taking notes at meetings, and found it quite helpful.

Trying to make a commercial product out of it did not turn out successfully, but then again, the effort put into it was not very strong either.

Mind you, it was a concept including a dictation hardware product developed and produced by ourselves, called "Voicetrap", as well as a booklet with pre-printed forms for note-taking. Using the concept forced you not to overlook anything, when for instance taking notes at a meeting.

Do we want to be so disciplined? I really don't think so, I believe we have all got our own personal methods, and should stick to them.

When I see the president of the board of our Danish company and the way he takes the minutes at our board meetings, I can be nothing but very impressed. Not about the way he takes the minutes, because you can scarcely see him do anything, but about the result you get in writing a few days later.

At the meeting he just scribbles down a few points it seems, but the two or three pages of concentrated information you get later, is just to the point. It is as if he has recorded the meeting, not to miss out the details.

I know for a fact that he after the meeting dictates the minutes based on his scribbled notes.

Practising is the key to all success and good results.

He has only been with us for about fifteen years, so I suppose he has invented a few personal tricks on how to keep track of the details and not to forget anything.

By the way, we are developing and producing sophisticated equipment for making recordings in court rooms and all kinds of meetings, with built in solutions for transcribing. It seems, however, that for taking minutes at meetings, each person prefers to use his or her own methods.

It came to my mind as this Sunday is very grey and snowy, and I'm in the office with my son-in-law. He is struggling to put the last touches to the marketing plan which has to be presented to the board tomorrow. He is the marketing manager of our company, and as such he is responsible for the marketing plan. It should, of course, have been ready months ago and been part of the input for the budget for this year, and not presented at the first board meeting in February.

To put words on paper is for some people easier then for others, but I believe it is still an important part of the day to day business to be able to do so.

Improving your skills in this respect can only be achieved through a lot of blood, sweat and tears.

After having gone through his marketing plan I must admit it is not at all bad, much better than last year's.

Shabby thoughts in the night   Jan Arnt 2017

The Nectie

For the first time in ten years, everyone attending our board meeting wore a tie.

Neither I, nor anyone else, have in any way indicated that a tie would be appreciated, but I suppose that there is some hidden factor which stops them turning up just wearing a shirt or a pullover.

I personally always wear a tie in the office and have done so as far back as I can remember.

It would be wrong for me to deny I'm conservative, although I cannot really see that wearing a tie should be a symbol of that.

I must admit that I am pleased to see them with a tie at the board-meeting, and that I would not mind at all if they continued wearing one.

Time heals most wounds they say, and I believe that we all to a certain extent have experienced that.

There are times, however, when you start wondering if it's really true.

IBM is now being focused upon, related to their activities during the last world war.

The Nazi Regime was supplied with technical equipment from IBM, or rather their German subsidiary.

We are talking about punch card machines, and I believe one can say that they were the data machines of that generation.

Now it has apparently been brought forward that the management of IBM knew that the machines supplied, and we are talking about big quantities, were used by the Nazis to keep record of the population and logically also to select those individuals whom, for reasons already known, they wanted to eliminate. It has been indicated that they supplied more than a billion punch cards every year throughout the war.

It will be interesting to see the outcome of the case, but merely the fact that these things have come to light now, fifty years later, is interesting.

The average price for a kilo of seafood in Norway is fifty-tree Norwegian kroner, about double the average in the common market.

Quite interesting for a fishing nation like Norway to top the list, but of such a margin they can be really proud.

Norwegians consumed a total of sixty-nine thousand tons of seafood last year, at a value of three point seven billion Norwegian kroner, or about three hundred million pounds.

The most incredible situation, however, is that Norway imports cod from Russia, and resells it to the EU without tax; not strange that we are making ourselves popular.

Why are the prices so high in Norway? I could express some thoughts about that, but will limit myself to one little factor, which I think may be one of the reasons.

Norway has reached new levels as regards the number of days per year that employees are off work. One whole month was the average in the year two thousand. What about that, is that another record? I have not the slightest idea what figures other countries are competing with, but as an employer I know that although you only pay half the cost and the state the other half, it is a heavy cost. Well, that is not the whole truth, as the taxes you pay are all together so high that the contribution from the state has already been paid many times over by the employer.

Turn it around and look at it from a different angle. If the above figures are correct, every twelfth person on the payroll is not present at all. We used to be well over one hundred in our business, in Norway alone, meaning that we had about ten non-existing people on the payroll.

Today we can in that respect be happy as we are only around thirty people, reducing the non-existing ones to about two and a half.

Records are something that Norway is very keen on, and particularly when it has to do with sport.

Liv Arnesen and her female partner were the first women to cross the South Pole on skies. Today they ended a two thousand seven- hundred-kilo-metre trip, which took them ninety days.

Design

Everything created by humans, whatever it is, has a touch of design. Even in ancient times I am convinced that anyone making, for instance, just a tool, automatically and without necessarily thinking about it, formed it so that it also became pleasing to the eye. Today design is much more than only form; it is a complete study of human interface and functionality.

I will not try to make the impression that I know much about design, but I have had the pleasure of working together with designers.

I have also made quite a few models of apparatus for various kinds of communication systems, which we developed and put into production in our company.

The Italian manufacturer of office machines, Olivetti, which our company in Norway represented from the beginning of the fifties to the end of the sixties, was at the forefront of industrial design in those days.

At the museum of modern art in New York, you can find quite a few of their machines produced in the fifties, as examples of the best industrial designs at the time.

During our period of co-operating with the Dutch company Philips in communication systems, I also had the pleasure of visiting their design department a few times.

In the period when we were most active in developing communication systems for Philips, the head of their design department in Eindhoven, was a Norwegian called Yran.

In Norway I think he will still be remembered as the one who made a fabulous drawing of a little Lapp boy.

The Lapps being an ethnic minority group in the north of the country. This picture was used internationally in endless presentations of Norway.

The way Philips presented their various designs was very impressive.

First imagine the vast product range that Philips represented and then the fact that all of them in a way should have a corporate image.

During presentations of suggested designs, you were seated at a round table with an opening in the middle. There were big boards with sketches all around the room, and I think Yran loved to do the presentations himself.

I remember him as a tall and not very slim fellow, walking around pointing with a stick at the sketches and arguing as to why they had chosen the various solutions.

Then, when the time came to present the actual model of a product, all the lights were dimmed, while spotlights were aimed at the circle in the middle of the table. Slowly, as if from nowhere, the actual product could be seen on a platform rising out of the centre of the table while slowly turning.

Needless to say, it was an impressive performance. But those were the good times when big money was spent in this sector.

I remember when his department was going to make the design of an intercom station at the beginning of the seventies.

Prior to the launch of the project, the so called IDC, International Development Committee, with around thirty members from all parts of the world, had several meetings to decide upon the general route to take.

Then something like twenty-five models were produced, displaying different suggested designs.

A final decision was taken by the IDC before the real work of industrializing the product started.

What made me think about this was the meeting we had this morning with a designer team from Denmark, which we hired to make a new dictation microphone.

They were here to present the first stage of their work after eight weeks.

Although in a much different fashion than Yran, they first presented a series of alternative routes to go, and then argued why they thought we would be best off with the one they finally suggested.

They had really got down to details about functionality and human interface as well, so we all felt we were taking a good decision when we gave them our go ahead.

St. Valentine

The story about St. Valentine is that a catholic priest protested against the Roman Emperor Claudius' ban on young men to get married. Married men make bad soldiers, the Emperor said. In all secrecy the priest, St. Valentine, who did not pay much attention to the ban, kept on marrying men until one day it came to the ear of the Emperor.

His reaction was short but not so sweet, because he sentenced the priest to death. While waiting for the execution to take place, the priest was put in jail, where he fell in love with the blind daughter of the warden.

According to the story, on February the fourteenth, the day before the execution, he sent a love-letter to his beloved, and signed it "from your Valentine".

The prisoner died, but the girl got her eyesight back.

I don't think it sounds like a lot, but five-thousand kilos of chocolate was given as presents in Norway last year on St. Valentine's Day. Further, some fifty thousand red roses and one million greeting cards changed hands. Not so bad for a country of four million people.

Love gifts of all kinds, and as mentioned more than a million cards are changing hands today in this country, with messages of love and friendship.

In the United States more than eighty million cards were sent last February fourteenth, while the Finns with a little more than five million inhabitants sent an incredible six million cards.

Having taken off from Oslo Airport on my way back home, I brought with me some souvenirs in form of a running nose, sore tonsils, and ear-ache.

Temperatures varying from minus twenty to plus five, and children coming back from their different kindergartens every day with God knows what kinds of things and with constantly running noses, is too much for someone having settled down in a milder, sunnier climate.

My wife has spent the last weekend in Geneva with her family and we are supposed to meet at the airport in Alicante and drive home together.

According to her schedule, she will land one hour before me, and will be waiting in the little <u>café</u> where we normally have our coffee when she takes me there for my trips to Norway.

The three and three quarter hour flight from Oslo went very fast this time, as I had the pleasure of sitting beside a young man working for the same airline we were flying with.

I have always been fascinated by planes, and now I got a good chance to pick up some knowledge about a side of it which I knew nothing about, as he was working in the cargo department.

Luckily enough, when they announced the tax free sales, I was reminded about St. Valentine, and used the opportunity to buy a present for my wife.

We landed a little more than half an hour late in pretty cold and wet weather, something which, after all, can be expected at this time of year.

My wife had brought along all the ingredients, fresh from Switzerland, for a cheese fondue, an excellent meal in weather like this.

Confused thoughts

Autumn

Nothing is like a September day in the Norwegian mountains, if the sun is shining that is. It is important that the sun be shining, as only then do you get the right impression of the fantastic autumn colours. Over the years until I stopped shooting ptarmigans about ten years ago, I must have spent many months in the mountains all together at this time of the year. The shooting season used to start the first of September, more or less the time when the green leaves turn to yellow and red on the dwarf birches.

Our family cabin, which a long time ago was taken over by my brother and sister, is situated almost exactly at one thousand meters above sea level. It is built on a little peninsula in a rather big lake, and on a sunny day with no wind, you can see the mountainside with its magnificent colours, mirrored in the lake.

We always used to be five or six friends together for long weekends, and we normally brought my two English Setters and a couple of Pointers along.

To see them searching for the birds and pointing when they find them is an experience so full of emotions that it cannot be described. They can stand pointing for quite a while, as they paralyse the birds. If one of the dogs is pointing, the other ones if they are nearby will ideally come up behind the one pointing to support its stand.

Only when you walk up behind the dog yourself and give it a signal, it will advance a few steps.

If things go according to plan, only one or two birds from the covey will take wing before the dog comes to a stop and points again, while you shoot.

Then there is a new signal and the same procedure repeats itself.

Well, this is if everything goes according to plan, something which seldom happens, but for someone having experienced it, it is a great moment in life.

Sitting in our dining room like we do for dinner almost every evening, I am facing a picture given to me by my family for my sixtieth birthday.

It was painted in the forties by a rather well known Norwegian painter.

It contains the autumn colours I am referring to, and they gave it to me so that I, living in Spain, would be reminded of Norway.

Underneath the picture, the front of a Norwegian cupboard from the middle of the nineteenth century is placed. Its original colours match one hundred percent the picture above, and the two together against the white wall with the fireplace underneath is something I treasure very much.

It has all to do with the fact that up north, the four seasons are so distinct, and each of them represents something very special.

Colours are one thing, and so is the emotion that goes with them. When I listen to "Spring" by the composer Edward Grieg, I can almost feel that spring is here. The snow is melting and the bare trees are getting their new shoots.

When you listen to his "In the Hall of the Mountain King", you can practically see the Norwegian mountains in front of your eyes, even if you are sitting in the South of Spain. Grieg is only one of many I think, who has this refined way of expressing music, making it resemble the country of the composer.

Finland's, Sibelius, has the same ability to do so, and to most Finns he will give the same feeling as Grieg does to Norwegians.

Afterthoughts

Buying House

In Norway we have the saying: "all good things come in threes". For quite a long time my daughter and son-in-law have been looking for a house. They are the owner of, and live in, a lovely flat situated very centrally in Oslo. They have plenty of space, even for me when I every now and then make a business trip to the country.

They bought this flat a few years ago, after having sold the previous smaller one.

Their two boys, my grandsons, two and a half and four and a half, go to their respective kindergartens, and I think what drives their parents more than anything else is thinking what will happen when the older one starts school in about two years' time.

Anyway, the best way you can get hold of a house is looking at the advertisements in the newspapers, and then visit the ones on offer that you want to take a closer look at.

The main newspaper is filled with such advertisements every day, mentioning the assessment price and the time when you can pay them a visit.

Half an hour out of the city, prices are between half and one third of those nearer the centre.

Well, my daughter it seems, has made up her mind on behalf of herself and my son-in-law that they, if possible, should find a house closer to the city, as that is where she grew up herself, and that is where they would like the boys to be brought up I suppose.

The calculation of how to finance the purchase of a house is going on all the time, the key factor being what they can get for their flat.

The last few times I have been in Oslo, I joined them having a closer look at some houses.

I'm, of course, very reluctant to give advice of any sort, but I don't think it is difficult to read my mind. I find the prices horrendous, but I can only trust that they, when finally taking a decision, will be able to feed themselves and the kids, besides paying the mortgage on the house.

The last time I was there we went to look, only from the outside, at a house which had been advertised once before.

That happens very seldom these days, as almost all houses are sold when first advertised.

People take a look, and then, if they are really interested in buying, they make a binding offer.

The real estate agent informs the owner and all other interested parties about the bid at hand, and hopes for a higher one to come.

It really is nerve-racking when you are in the bidding position, and you must be prepared that all of a sudden you have the highest bid and that the house is yours. The law giving you no option to change your mind.

From outside the house was very special, looking like it was built of natural stone. Not at all a typical Norwegian style house, but the plot had a fantastic view of the Oslo fjord. The garage was only a meter from the most heavily trafficked road up to the Holmenkollen ski jump, but despite that, we decided to have a closer look.

To make a long story short, they actually went up a couple of times and found that this could be their big chance. It might be the house of a lifetime. No bid had been made so far, so they decided to give it a try.

As the indicated price was far above their economic possibilities, they started off with a low bid, not really believing that they had much of a chance. The next day a higher bid came in, but only one.

The owner, whom they later got to know, and who had to sell the house to clear up some economic matters with the tax man, refused to sell for the price offered, and wanted to do another round of advertising.

This was done, but even then no new bids turned up.

I thought, and said so, that this type of house did not necessarily appeal to Norwegians with the kind of money in question. I may well have been right, because at the end of the day, or rather today, they made a final bid, not much higher than the first one, and got the house.

Next time I go to Oslo I may well be staying at a new address.

I was thinking about this when I came back from the garage having traded in the old Ford Fiesta for the new four wheel drive Hyundai Santa Fe.

My wife has had the third of some very tough and crucial meetings at the town hall, so when I got home and she told me that today's had been extremely positive, I thought it right to say: "all good things come in threes".

Thought Tom

ID number

Building and selling houses, you enter in many ways into a personal relationship with your customers. It is all a matter of how you look at things of course, but at least those of us living in the area, see it as our responsibility to go a little further than just finishing the house, giving the key to the customer and collecting the money.

Put yourself in the customer's place, or maybe you already have the experience of having built a house in Spain.

I am not talking about the experience of building the house as such, because that in itself can be quite a challenge. I am talking about what happens when you finally get the key to the house, or even before that, when you want to plan what furniture, lamps, curtains etc., you want to buy.

Where do you find the shops and how do you arrange the deliveries if the house is not yet finished.

We normally talk about people who are here just for holidays, not living here permanently.

Almost all customers come from abroad and very few speak Spanish, something which may be a problem as in many shops they are not very familiar with foreign languages.

Apart from all official papers related to the house, contracts will have to be made for electricity, gas and telephone.

All costs involved with these contracts will automatically be charged to your bank account, which means you will have to open one as a start.

To be able to pay your taxes you must have a NIE, which is an identification number, and when buying most types of capital goods they will also ask you for it.

All this has to be arranged, and most people will need help.

We normally advise our customers to engage the services of a solicitor, who apart from making sure that all the papers in conjunction with the house are in order, can also help with other things.

Well, we have an arrangement through our sales office, so customers who do not think it necessary to engage a solicitor, are helped with most of the practicalities.

Today I have been updating myself about furniture shops in the area, something I thought was necessary, as I have not been looking for furniture since we moved into our own house quite a few years ago.

Some Norwegian customers are here for just over a week with their two children.

They knew that their house would not be ready upon their arrival, and we arranged for them to rent a flat in the urbanization.

The husband and wife have only been here once before last autumn, when they over a weekend decided to buy a half-finished house in a group of eight.

For the kids, this is their first time in Spain, and as they are eight and eleven they are, of course, curious about the place.

Before lunch I think we visited about six shops and I must say I was impressed with the selection of furniture they had.

The idea was for me to show them the shops, enabling them over the next few days to go deeper into the matter and make their purchases.

We have made arrangements with them to get the shops to deliver what they eventually buy, in week thirteen, as we are then sure that the house will be finished.

The shops will call our sales office before delivering, and we will see to it that the furniture is put into their house, as they will only be back at a later time.

We will also arrange for the insurance.

Now it remains to be seen how they get on with their purchasing in the coming days, something I think will work out very well, as they are quite international and have already started learning Spanish.

Green fee

Incredible forty-eight million five hundred thousand tourists visited Spain last year, they informed us today. Since the total number of inhabitants of Spain is forty-five million, it means that the country is visited by more people than live here. I don't know what proportion of tourists visit Andalucia, but we certainly feel the pressure in our area. Never in all the years I have been here, have I seen so much building going on everywhere.

This means that the economy is good in Europe at the moment and for us, who in all modesty build and sell houses, it is important that it continue this way.

One thing we feel, however, is that prices in general are going up. Spain is not at all a country where you can expect to live cheaply in the future, and why should one think so.

The standard of living is generally high, and I suppose they very soon will level with most other countries in the Common Market, if they are not already there.

We have seen foreigners in our community, who invested here in the middle of the eighties, having to leave, as their pensions could not keep abreast with the increase in prices.

As we are golfers we carefully check the prices for eventual membership at golf clubs and what you have to pay in green fees.

First of all, as far as we can understand, new golf developments do not offer membership, as it is possibly more interesting money-wise, to let people play on a green fee basis only. Green fees vary from five thousand pesetas up to well over twenty thousand per person for a round of golf, which means I would guess, an average of around eight thousand.

For two people whose main hobby is golf, and who stay here permanently, this is quite a budget. For people coming for a holiday on a package tour where golf is included, I suppose that prices are more than acceptable.

Imagine that two people want to play three times a week, for let's say thirty or forty weeks a year, and what that will amount to.

As we are members of our club, and pay a yearly fee which we feel is acceptable, we are very fortunate.

The only snag is that our club is one hour's drive from where we live.

This spring two new golf courses will open in our area, and a third will open late next year. None of them will be arranged as a club with membership, and listen to this:

One of them is offering a special deal where one person can play as much as he or she wants per year; in other words as if you were a member, at a price of nine hundred and fifty thousand pesetas. For a couple that means almost two million pesetas a year, and imagine what that would end up at if it were a family with kids going for the sport.

It's the market that decides the price of course, but some obviously think that trees can grow into heaven?

Sweden is a country which has made golf an every man's sport.

For the price of one and a half green fees in Spain, you can in Sweden get a deal including hotel, meal and green-fee.

France, where we go every now and then, also has a totally different price policy, making it a pleasure to both stay and play without feeling that you've been robbed.

In a golf magazine I just read that one named club in the Marbella area, is seeing their paying members leave the club as they can no longer afford to play golf.

The author of the article made the conclusion that for price reasons many foreign golfers living in Spain will have to quit and maybe take up bowling instead.

May someone prevent that from happening to us.

Short Stories

The heading and the date were already there. They were written exactly 11 years ago today, Monday February 19th, not 2001. I have had great challenges transferring all these "Thoughts" from the old computer to the one I am using today.

The fact is that I never looked at them since I wrote them, one every day for almost two months, from the first of January 2001.

In other words, they were not forgotten, they were just kept in the old machine, which I still have on the left side of my desk.

It was a very advanced and expensive laptop in those days. However, after some years the screen packed up.

There was no way it could be mended in the area where we live, so what else could I do than to buy a separate screen. This worked fine until I got my new Dell a few years ago.

It is something about the format that makes the transfer of files complicated. I had to send them as mails from one computer to the other.

Why I kept writing "Thoughts" only up until and including the 18th of February 2001, I don't remember, but from that day on I only made a few notes about daily events, until the end of the month. On some days I didn't even do that.

The reason they have surfaced now is that I am trying to tidy up my writings.

Through the nineties, mostly concentrated around the middle of the decade, I wrote close to a hundred short stories, which I am now getting translated from Norwegian into English.

In light of this I thought that I should also keep track of, and tidy up, the ones from the first almost two months of 2001 as well. In those days I wrote them in English and as you have seen they are called "Thoughts".

I have decided to call my short stories "Reflections" which I think is a more apt title.

I have no plans for what I eventually will do with them, apart from tidying them up. Maybe, after having done so, I may come up with a plan.

So what to do with the unfinished last 10 days of February 2001?

Well, as I so far have no plans for the missing link, I can only dwell on my few notes taken on those days in 2001.

As always, the weather is important, and it rained heavily 11 years ago today. Although not very pleasant for golf, we say it is good for the farmers, especially in this part of the world as they always suffer from lack of water.

Politics seem to have prevented the great idea of transferring water from the river Ebro down to Andalucia. The great river Ebro passes the city of Tortosa, about a 6 or 7 hour drive from here towards Barcelona.

There has been a lot written in the papers about the building of new hotels in our area. In fact, it has become reality as well, as at least four new ones are under construction. However, as they are getting well under way you start wondering what the planners are thinking, or rather who is responsible.

What about the infrastructure in general? There seem to be little focus on the fact that new upgraded roads, shopping areas, and all types of facilities are needed as well, making the area more attractive to tourism.

Debates are going on in the papers about the problems of infrastructure but it is impossible for outsiders to understand what the plans for the future are.

Looking closer at my notes for the remaining days of February 2001, I have come to the conclusion that I had rather forget trying to write about them. It would not be in real time, so I will stick with the 51 first days of 2001. That includes the next one, slightly modified, covering February 20th 2001, which I discovered by accident in another file in my old computer when trying to tidy things up.

The Skilift

Most English papers sold in Spain are printed here. That is at least what is happening today in 2012. I don't know if it was also the case in 2001, and I don't remember if my notes taken on that day 11 years ago were taken from English or Spanish newspapers or from television. That, of course, has nothing to do with the content of the information itself.

Youngsters in the UK are now topping the list of young people hurting themselves while under the influence of alcohol, and this mainly happens at weekends.

Apparently parents are unaware of where their sons and daughters are and what they are doing. It's also claimed that youngsters down to only eight years of age are smoking.

I suppose there is a first time in life for most of us to try various challenges but if parents have lost control, there is of course a great chance that one thing will lead to another.

I will not dwell further on this subject, only state my opinion that parents must take most of the responsibility for this and other happenings.

This reminds me of a personal experience many years ago. I am not proud of it at all, and it is not the way it should work, but I was in my early twenties and suppose I felt that what I was doing was right at the time.

Queueing for the lift at a downhill slope outside Oslo together with some friends, a young boy, I would think of around 12 or 13, just put himself at the front of the queue every time he had finished a run.

To be able to do so he could not enter directly in front. He had to pass all the other people in the queue, and he did that every time.

No one seemed to bother too much as it was only himself and a friend, but as the queue was long and they passed us at least 2 or 3 times for every run the rest of the queue had, I stopped him and told him he had to respect the queue.

He ignored my gentle advice and forced his way to the front.

The next time I stopped him, I told him this was his last chance to behave.

Again he refused to behave and needless to say, I built up a temper.

When he passed me the third time, I stopped him, said something about having given him a chance to behave and took my ski stick and pushed it hard into one of his skis.

The result was that the back of the ski split.

Then I said something like. "Now you can go home to your parents and tell them that this happened because they never taught you how to behave".

Crying the boy left with his friend.

As I said, I am not proud of what I did, and I do not suppose my intention was to split his ski. The ones witnessing the happening all thought it would have taught him a much needed lesson.

The downhill skis in those days were still made of wood. Doing the same today would never split a modern ski.

As a Rotarian I am proud to hear, it is now real time 2012, that tuberculosis has been as good as eradicated. At every meeting we have had since the late eighties, we have put ten kroner each in a plastic tube for the purpose of helping reach this goal.

I remember there were millions of cases every year back then. In 2010 a total of 360,000 caught the illness, and in 2011 there were only 60.000 cases.

We saw a documentary from somewhere in Africa where Rotarians gave two drops of some liquid to each child, enough to prevent them from getting the decease.

In the midst of all the challenges we see in the world, it is nice to witness that actions like this one can help create wonders.

The four solar seasons.

Spring:
The sun is eager to make its way high up in the sky and inspire all living things to reach for it.

Summer:
The sun wanders directly across the sky, in the middle of the neutral zone between spring and autumn.

Autumn:
The sun is pulled down towards the horizon, into autumns's inevitable embrace.

Winter:
The sun lets go of its promise of warmth and settles for its illuminating clarity.

GM.